PENGUIN BOOKS

DON CAMILLO MEETS
HELL'S ANGELS

Giovanni Guareschi lived at Parma,
near the River Po, where he was born
in 1908. As he himself recounted, his
parents wished him to be a naval
engineer: consequently he studied
law, made a name as a sign-board
painter, and among other jobs, gave
mandolin lessons. His father had a
heavy black moustache under his
nose: Giovanni grew one just like it.
He always wore it and was proud of
it. He was not bald, wrote eight books,
and was five feet ten inches tall. 'I also
have a brother,' Guareschi said, adding,
'but I prefer not to discuss him. And I
have a motor-cycle with four cylinders,
an automobile with six cylinders,
and a wife and two children.'

As a young man he drew cartoons for
Bartoldo. When the war came he was
arrested by the political police for
howling in the streets all one night. In
1943 he was captured by the Germans
at Alessandria and adopted the slogan:
'I will not die even if they kill me.'
Back in Italy after the war he became
editor-in-chief of *Candido* at Milan.
He scripted a film, *People Like This*.

Giovanni Guareschi died in 1968.

GIOVANNI GUARESCHI

Don Camillo meets
Hell's Angels

Translated by L. K. Conrad

PENGUIN BOOKS

Penguin Books Ltd, Harmondsworth
Middlesex, England
Penguin Books Australia Ltd, Ringwood,
Victoria, Australia

This translation is from *Don Camillo e i giovanni d'oggi* first published in the
U.S.A. under the title *Don Camillo Meets the Flower Children*, 1969
Published in Great Britain, under the title *Don Camillo meets Hell's Angels*, 1970
Published in Penguin Books, 1972

Copyright © Rizzoli Editore, 1969
Translation Copyright © Farrar, Straus & Giroux, Inc., 1969
This edition copyright © Victor Gollancz Ltd., 1970

Made and printed in Great Britain by
Hunt Barnard Printing Ltd, Aylesbury, Bucks.

Set in Monotype Baskerville

Contents

Don Camillo and the lost sheep

PEPPONE's Achilles' heel was called Michele, a brutish youth with hands like shovels and hair so long that it made one think of those acacia trees which, pummelled daily, are reduced to fat trunks capped with silly-looking balls of foliage. This Michele moved about on a grotesque motorcycle equipped with saddle bags adorned with studs and fringes, cowboy-style, and he costumed himself in a leather jacket on which was painted a white skull and the word 'Venom'.

Michele, called Venom, was the youngest of Comrade Peppone's sons, and the only longhair in town. In spite of this, he kept things moving, because he had the brains to use his buffalo strength devilishly efficiently. Venom headed the Valley's few longhairs, and when he and his gang toured the country, the ground shook.

Another important change in Don Camillo's parish: old Piletti's pharmacy had been taken over by a young lady from the big city who had moved into the town nestled on the bank of the great river Po, bringing her husband, Bognoni, who was a doctor.

As for Peppone, he had transformed his Communist Party headquarters into a huge emporium where he sold all manner of cars, motorcycles, and electrical appliances. Most of the capital to start the venture was put up by the cell comrades, persuaded by Peppone's line of reasoning: 'If the working class today needs cars, washing machines, televisions, refrigerators, and so forth, we should sell them to ourselves. That way the profit stays in the hands of the working class because the shop's earnings will be divided among its clients.'

Neither Doctor Bognoni nor his wife, the pharmacist Comrade Jole, approved of this shop. Both of them had been commended as activists of great efficaciousness by the regional commune, and welcomed enthusiastically into the directorate of the commune. It seemed to both of them that the enterprise could only serve to stimulate bourgeois tendencies on the part of the workers, and rob them of all revolutionary zeal.

'Now see here, Comrade Botazzi,' Bognoni had said to Peppone, 'you are giving the people illusions of prosperity and forgetting that revolution can only be fomented from the people's sufferings!'

'Nothing's to stop the people from suffering when they have Fiats, televisions, fridges, and washing machines,' Peppone countered, since he himself was a man of the people and knew them well.

Forced to swallow the pill for the time being, the two Bognonis bitterly retreated to plan reprisals against Peppone, waiting for a propitious moment to launch a full-fledged offensive.

Before long, the opportunity presented itself. Venom and his gang, caught in Castelleto's dance hall one night and ejected as undesirables, took the dance hall by storm and relinquished it only after they'd made off with every pair of trousers there. The episode sat particularly badly because Venom, that same night, dragged himself up one of the two very tall high-tension scaffolds that supported cables crossing the Po river, fastened a long rope to the crossbar, and hung out the entire booty of fifty-seven pairs of trousers which flapped in the breeze like a ship's bunting. Next day, the crowds gathered by the river to enjoy the spectacle of the trousers billowing in the wind.

The Bognonis called a town meeting to denounce Venom as a foul example of bourgeois hooliganism, the shame of the town, and ended on this sour note: 'If Comrade Botazzi brings up his children this way, how can he pretend to formulate new canons for the growth of the Party?' They added that the cause of the working people was not to be served by tending shop or sitting around selling electrical gadgets.

Peppone's first idea was to thrash both Bognonis. Then he thought it over and decided to send the regional commune a detailed report, asking for an immediate reply.

That evening, Don Camillo, bursting with glee, went inside his parish church to have a chat with the crucified Christ over the high altar. 'Lord,' he said, 'thank you for sowing the seeds of dissent in the fields of the enemies of God.'

'I do not bring darkness and discord,' the Christ replied. 'I can only bring light and peace. Don Camillo, your enemy also happens to be your neighbour, and your neighbour's troubles should be your troubles too.'

'Forgive me, Father,' said Don Camillo, 'but I just can't bring myself to feel sorry that Peppone has a longhaired son.'

'Don Camillo,' the Christ said, smiling, 'do not forget that even I, during my short earthly life, was a longhair!'

'Sir!' Don Camillo exclaimed with indignation. 'This young man isn't happy just to let his hair grow long and dress strangely. He also commits acts of violence and he is a tearaway!'

'Don Camillo,' the Christ reproved him, 'you give the sheep of your flock too easily to the wolves.'

'He's not a sheep of my flock!'

'You baptized him in the name of the Lord and that boy is a sheep of *my* flock!'

Don Camillo didn't get a chance to answer because at that moment Peppone came into the church. There were storm warnings in his face and Don Camillo dragged him into the rectory.

9

'Comrade Mayor,' he said when they were inside in the dining room, 'have you finally repented your sins? Speak freely: God alone hears you, not Comrade Bognoni.'

'You and your blasted Latinisms!' Peppone roared. 'Would you mind telling me what *cum grano salis* means?'

'It depends on the context in which it is used,' Don Camillo answered.

'The context in which it was used was that I reported to the regional commune what those two louts said about me in public, and the commune replied that I must act *cum grano salis.*'

Don Camillo guffawed, which drove Peppone into a fury. 'These damnable intellectuals, they'll be the ruin of the Party! What's the matter with plain Italian? Now that even the priests have discarded Latin, what provokes the Party's petty functionaries to use it?'

'Comrade,' Don Camillo explained very patiently, 'might it be that they were advising you to proceed with tact, prudence, diplomacy, and intelligence, when everybody knows that you haven't even a nodding acquaintance with those virtues? They refer to that microscopic grain of salt which they hope you have tucked away inside that fat head of yours, and they are advising you to take advantage of it.'

'Poppycock!' Peppone exploded. 'I'll show them what they can do with their *grano salis*. I'm going to stuff the honourable doctors cum grano peppers and watch them turn green! How can I help it if my son is a drop-out? Anyhow, if that hoodlum has the face to come home, I'll murder him!'

'Fine idea,' Don Camillo approved. 'It's much easier to kill off sons than educate them.'

'Who said anything about killing off?' Peppone huffed. 'I mean that if I ever get my hands on him, I'll show him what kind of welts a nice fresh stick of wood makes.'

'You're better off killing him, Comrade. Prosperity

has turned you into a pot of lard. If he so much as throws a fist at you, he'll do you in.'

'Are you suggesting that if I hit him, he'll turn against me?'

'If he really is your son, yes.'

'That he is, unfortunately,' Peppone sighed, dejectedly.

At that moment Comrade Smilzo came in at a dead run, all out of breath.

'Now what's going on here, in my rectory?' Don Camillo barked. 'Is this a meeting of the local Party cell, or what?'

'If the Pope himself can receive the Soviet Foreign Minister in the Vatican, certainly an insignificant parish priest such as yourself can receive a couple of comrades from the local Communist cell,' Smilzo replied, adding: 'or do you consider yourself more important than the Pope?'

'What's the matter?' Peppone asked Smilzo.

'Chief,' Smilzo explained, 'your son Michele broke into the pharmacy and forced Comrade Jole to drink half a bottle of castor oil. Then he stormed over to the hospital and made Doctor Bognoni drink the rest of it!'

Peppone turned white and sank into a convenient chair. 'I'm ruined,' he moaned. 'Castor oil! Now they'll accuse me of raising a Fascist son! The unholy wretch! Of all things to make them drink, how *could* he choose castor oil!'

Meanwhile, Brusco had invaded the rectory too, bringing further news. 'No, Chief, it wasn't castor oil. It was a bottle of cod-liver oil.'

'Oh, thank God,' Peppone sighed. 'At least they won't be able to make a political issue out of it. But I swear I'm going to beat up that hooligan! You two come along with me and step in only if he tries anything. You'll see how Comrade Peppone handles things!'

The three comrades ran out leaving Don Camillo to turn his eyes toward heaven; spreading his arms out helplessly, he said, 'Lord, one of your sheep is lost, and the wolves are circling round him. I don't know where to dig him out. Whatever can I do?'

'It is written: *Pulsate et aperietur vobis.* So, my friend, go and knock,' the distant voice of the Christ suggested.

Instead Don Camillo took to pacing up and down the room, since he didn't understand the Christ's meaning. Therefore, when he heard a knock at the door, he went to answer it.

Venom came in, his hair rumpled and hiding his face. The young rebel was quite agitated. 'Father,' he said, 'my old man's after me to break my bones into tiny pieces.'

Don Camillo looked at him disgustedly. 'Do you mean to say that, in spite of those hams, you're afraid of an old pot of lard like your father?'

'Of course! If he catches me, there's nothing I can do except take it from him. I can't fight my old man!'

Don Camillo studied the tearaway with less disgust. 'Don't you know what you've got him into, what with your giving the Bognonis the purge?'

'It wasn't what they said about me that earned them the purge; it was what they said about the old man that set me off. Come on, Don Camillo, help a fellow, won't you?'

'The house of God is open to the sinner who repents his evil ways.'

Venom puffed out his huge chest and clenched his fists. 'I'm damned if I'll repent,' he shouted. 'It's those two quacks who are sinning, not me!'

'If you feel that way about it,' Don Camillo replied evenly, 'either you leave here immediately, or, if you decide to stay, you will have to pay.'

'That's no problem; I'll be glad to,' Venom all but shouted.

When Don Camillo told him what the price would be, the youth replied that, rather than pay it, he would let his throat be cut.

'Then leave,' Don Camillo ordered.

Venom headed for the door, but halfway there, he stopped and turned around. 'Father, you are asking an ugly thing.'

'Take it or leave it. Here we have fixed prices, no discounts.'

Venom came back, sat down, and, gritting his teeth, paid up. Afterwards, he shook himself off. 'Father, you've ruined me for life.'

'Well, this is not exactly my line of work, but it's not a bad job at that,' Don Camillo answered. 'Even shaved bald, you look a hundred per cent better.'

While Don Camillo put away the electric razor and swept up the mountain of dirty hair, Venom took a mirror out of his pocket and scrutinized the damage. 'Scalped like this, I'm an absolute nobody now,' he said with anguish. The truth was, he felt like Samson after Delilah had finished with his hair, completely weakened, because the source of his strength was in his hair. 'I won't be able to lift up my head in public ever again,' Venom sighed. 'I'll have to leave town.'

'Where will you go?'

'I've already got a place: I've been drafted, so I'm off to be a soldier.'

Don Camillo was stunned. 'But I thought you were supposed to be the head of that group of so-called conscientious objectors?'

'True, but the only reason I did it was because going into the Army meant having my head shaved. Now that I'm as bald as a worn tyre it's no longer a moral issue.'

'I see,' Don Camillo gurgled. 'Now go on and get yourself something to eat in the kitchen and then go to bed. The guest room is on the top floor. And sleep well. Nobody's going to bother you.'

Don Camillo dashed into the church to confide in the Christ. 'Lord, I do thank you. The good shepherd has found his lost sheep just as you said.'

'Yes, Don Camillo; however, I said nothing about the

good shepherd shearing the lost sheep once he was found.'

'This is a technical detail which is the shepherd's prerogative, not God's. Render unto God what is God's, render unto the shepherd what is his; isn't that one of the things you decreed?'

'No, Don Camillo, but it's the right idea.'

Venom stayed for a week, hidden in Don Camillo's house, and passed the time chopping up enough wood for the entire winter.

The eighth day, Peppone appeared, in a frenzy. 'Michele's induction notice came today,' he moaned, 'and I don't know where he's vanished to, the wretch. If he doesn't present himself on time, they'll hunt him down as a deserter. Which means more trouble for me, if I don't find him.'

Don Camillo led Peppone through the kitchen to a tiny window overlooking the courtyard. There Peppone espied Venom chopping wood. Peppone's jaw dropped. 'Why, he's bald as a vulture!' he exclaimed.

'Right you are,' Don Camillo said. 'I've persuaded him to study for the priesthood.'

Peppone jumped. 'Never!' he shouted. 'Rather than see him waste his life, I'll let him come home. I swear I won't say a word to him, even though it's his fault those blasted Bognonis are trying to even the score with me by founding an autonomous Maoist cell.'

'Well, all right,' Don Camillo reluctantly agreed. 'It's too bad, though. It sounded so nice: "Brother Venom, God's own sheep". '

'There's no place among the Botazzis for sheep!' Peppone declared.

'Oh, yes,' Don Camillo said nastily, 'I almost forgot that once upon a time, Comrade, you had a sign painted over your front door: "Better to live one day as a lion than a hundred years as a sheep". '

'You and your confounded memory can go to hell!' Peppone roared as he left the rectory. 'The account between me and you isn't settled yet!'

'We'll settle it,' Don Camillo reassured him. 'Mao permitting, that is.'

The great river flowed on, peaceful and indifferent. It was a day like any other . . . but different.

The secret of St Antony the Abbot

A LITTLE red Fiat pulled up at the fountain in the rectory courtyard, and a thin young man got out, dressed in grey, with owlish eyeglasses and a leather briefcase under his arm. Don Camillo was in his study at his desk, reading the *Evening Gazette* with one eye, while with the other he spied on the courtyard. Seeing the young man, Don Camillo clenched his fists.

As soon as he heard the knock, he growled ungraciously: 'Come in.'

The young man opened the door, said hello, and presented Don Camillo with an envelope.

'I can't buy anything,' Don Camillo muttered without even raising his head from the newspaper.

'I'm not here to sell anything,' the man replied. 'My name is Don Francesco, the assistant assigned to you by the Curia, and this is my letter of introduction.'

Don Camillo squared him off. 'Seeing you dressed like that, young man, I took you for a travelling salesman. Considering you have come to introduce yourself to a poor old parish priest, you might have found it suitable to dress like a priest yourself.'

The little priest, who was the nervous type, paled; and Don Camillo proceeded to read the letter.

'Fine,' Don Camillo said, folding the letter and reinserting it in the envelope. 'Then you were sent here in order to show me how to be a priest.'

'No, Father, just to remind you that we're living not in 1669 but in 1969.'

Don Camillo pulled a large yellow handkerchief out of his pocket and made a knot in it. 'Now that I've made this reminder to myself, you may go,' he said.

The little priest lost his calm. 'Reverend Father! It was the Papal Curia that sent me here, and here I shall stay!' he squeaked, planting himself rigidly in front of the desk.

'In that case,' Don Camillo said calmly, 'let us profit by the occasion for a game of cards. Do you play One Hundred and Four?'

'No,' the little priest answered through clenched teeth.

There were some old decks of cards on the desk. Don Camillo selected one, grasped it between his powerful hands, and in one smooth movement ripped it in two.

The little priest was not impressed. 'I do play this game,' he said. 'But with much less effort.' Gathering up another deck of cards from the desk, he very calmly proceeded to tear the fifty-two cards in half, one by one.

'Now I have one hundred and four just like your pile, Father,' he said afterwards, smiling.

Don Camillo nodded his approval. 'However,' he said, pointing to the two piles of shredded playing cards, 'I know how to make you eat all two hundred and eight pieces.'

This was the Don Camillo of the rough and stormy past, and the little priest turned deathly pale. 'See here,' he babbled, '*I was sent here*. Now if it's me personally that you don't like . . .'

'You or anybody else, it makes no difference. Since His

Excellency has decreed that I have need of an assistant, I will obey him. It was gracious of you to remind me that we are living in 1969, not 1669, and I return your courtesy by reminding you that I am the parish priest here. Your room is ready. You may use it to refresh yourself and to dress yourself as a priest. Mufti is not allowed here during working hours.'

Old Desolina showed the little priest up to the guest room and Don Camillo ran to confer with the crucified Christ over the high altar in his church.

The fact was, in Don Camillo's church there was still an old-fashioned altar, at which Don Camillo persisted in celebrating the Mass in Latin. And the faithful continued to take Communion kneeling in front of the altar rail with its little columns of marble painted to look like fake marble.

All the other churches of the diocese had substituted their altars with what Don Camillo not very respectfully chose to call 'buffet tables'; but inside Don Camillo's church, nothing had changed at all. It was precisely this intransigence that had caused the Curia, before it took more serious disciplinary steps, to send the stubborn parish priest of the Po valley a young priest whose job it would be to persuade the old reactionary to install the changes of the *Aggiornamento*.

Don Camillo stalked up and down the aisles of the church, trying to think how to begin what he wanted to say, when finally the Christ called to him.

'Don Camillo, what are you doing? Have you forgotten that the true power of a priest is his humility?'

'Lord,' Don Camillo exclaimed, 'I have never forgotten it, and here I am, prostrate before you, the humblest of all your servants.'

'Don Camillo, it is very easy to humble oneself before God. Your own God became a man and humbled himself before all men.'

'Lord,' Don Camillo howled in anguish, stretching out his arms, 'why must I destroy everything?'

'You're not destroying anything. "Change the picture's frame and the picture stays the same." Or do you consider the frame more important than the picture?'

Don Camillo looked unconvinced.

'Don Camillo: if a cassock does not make a monk, then most certainly it does not make a priest. Or do you maintain that you are more a minister of God than that young man simply because you wear a cassock and he wears a jacket and trousers? Don Camillo, do you maintain that your God is so ignorant that he understands only Latin? Don Camillo: this stucco, this painted wood, this marble, these ancient words are not true faith.'

'Lord,' Don Camillo answered humbly, 'they are tradition, though; the memory, the path followed for so many years, the poetry . . .'

'All very pretty things, none of which have anything to do with faith. Don Camillo, you love these things because they remind you of your past and because you feel they are yours, almost a part of you. True humility consists in renouncing what one loves best.'

Don Camillo bowed his head and said, 'I will obey, my Lord.' But the Christ smiled because he could read into Don Camillo's heart.

The new priest was full of enthusiasm. His motto was '*Demysticise!*' That is, clean out all that was mere tinsel and served only to nourish superstition. But he was trying to work discreetly and avoid irritating Don Camillo. For his part, Don Camillo followed quietly along behind him, albeit with gritted teeth.

At a certain point, Don Camillo put his foot down. 'We will remove the altar,' he said in the same tone that he had offered to force the young priest to eat the torn cards, 'only when I find a suitable place to relocate it.'

This was hardly an easy chore. An altar crowned with a crucified Christ more than three yards tall is no knick-knack. But Don Camillo had a trick up his sleeve and he confided it to the Christ. 'Lord,' he explained, 'poor old Filotti's heirs have liquidated his entire estate.

The only thing that's left is the ancient, decrepit manor house with its private chapel, where I've always celebrated Mass once a year. They'll agree to part with everything for seven million lire. If I could have that chapel, I would move the altar and you with it over there. Here, you are a white elephant, and nobody can figure out what to do with you. Of course you will always be the Son of God Almighty, even if every image of you were to be destroyed, but I'll never allow them to throw you on that heap they've made of things they call useless.'

'Don Camillo,' the Christ admonished him, 'you're not talking about me. You're talking about a piece of painted wood.'

'Lord, my country is not a piece of coloured cloth called a flag. However, the flag of a country cannot be treated as if it were any old rag. And you are my flag, Sir. That chapel would be a good place for you, but even so, seven million lire are seven million lire. And where am I going to get that kind of money?'

'If you look where it is, you will find it,' the Christ answered, smiling enigmatically.

The little priest was champing at the bit. 'Father, even if we postpone the removal of the altar to some propitious time, we could begin the demystification by eliminating, for example, that awful painted doll of a St Antony.'

The truth was, the statue was an eyesore. Don Camillo had found it in its niche when he first came and had left it there, limiting his contact with it to an annual dusting.

The patron saint of the Valley's livestock, it seemed, had performed especially well in mitigating several serious anthrax epidemics between 1862 and 1914. He had then enjoyed prosperity and thousands of votive candles were lit at his feet daily. But once the anti-anthrax vaccination began to gain ground, the votive candles petered out, and now poor St Antony had to make do with the miserable allotment of ten tiny candles that Don Camillo had arranged in front of the niche. The niche itself was hidden behind an ancient oil vigil lamp.

Actually, Don Camillo had grown attached to his St Antony, but he accepted the little priest's suggestion. 'All right. Tomorrow you won't find it there.'

Est modus in rebus. He agreed to the eviction of St Antony, but not to liquidate him the way the little priest would have liked, with four blows of the hammer, after more than a hundred years of faithful service (one hundred and eight, to be exact, because the parish records showed that the statue had been given to the church in June of 1862 by a rich landowner, one Ferrazza). Helped by the bell-ringer, that same night Don Camillo dragged the St Antony down out of its niche and carted it into the store-room. During the removal, the saint's foot was bumped against a door handle and a chunk of his toes dropped off.

Don Camillo wanted to fix the damaged foot with some plaster before he went to bed, and so, while he was mixing up the plaster to apply to the chipped stucco, he noticed that, jutting out of the saint's broken foot, there was the toe of a black boot. And the boot was made not of plaster but of painted wood.

The lower part of the grey tunic that covered the saint down to his feet was cracked, and a light blow did the trick. This revealed something completely unexpected: St Antony wore, under his habit, breeches and boots with spurs.

Another blow did away with the upper part of the habit which came off like a crust, and behold, a piece of red shirt.

In a few moments, the crust of plaster covering the original wooden statue came clean away, and once stripped, St Antony turned out to be, unequivocally, the great Garibaldi.

The right arm still upheld in its fist a minuscule

crucifix; but it was clear that originally he had been holding a sword. The pilgrim's walking stick that the saint had held in his left hand was a handy camouflaging of a flag standard.

What was not clear was why Garibaldi had been masquerading as St Antony; however, it was not long before Don Camillo found that out too. Garibaldi's red shirt had a white spot on the left, in the shape of a heart. The heart wasn't wood but plaster, and Don Camillo tested its consistency with his knuckles. It was a fragile layer that shattered immediately, opening up a hole from which cascaded a tinkling shower of gold napoleons. Along with the napoleons, out came a leaflet folded in four.

On it was a story of the town, a little ridiculous perhaps, a little pathetic, but a piece of history.

In April of 1862, Garibaldi had visited the county seat, where he had been fêted like a demigod. The Garibaldi effigy in painted wood, the work of a local artisan, was a part of the festivities. But Garibaldi had delivered an extremely hard-line speech against the priests of Rome and against 'evil priests' in general to the Workers' Guild, and a certain Ferrazza, probably the head of the anticlerics of the town that later became Don Camillo's parish, had been so inspired by the speech that he bought the Garibaldi statue and had him transformed into the stucco St Antony. Then he gave him to the parish church.

These days, nobody understands that kind of joke, but there was a time when people got a laugh out of some very ferocious tricks. Here, the ferocity of the trick consisted not so much in bringing Garibaldi into the church and having him worshipped as a saint, but rather in filling up Garibaldi's chest with gold napoleons accompanied by this sarcastic note: *Dear priest (yes, priest, for there is gold here and only priests can detect gold, being so greedy for it!): Contrary to what you say, there is no Satan in the heart of Garibaldi. Instead, there is a precious treasure which you will certainly not refuse. Priest, if Masses are still being celebrated by the time you read this letter (and I doubt they will be), do celebrate a Mass for the repose of the soul of the anticleric Garibaldi-lover, Alberto Ferrazza, and use the napoleons to buy yourself a few nice banquets and toast the everlasting glory of Giuseppe Garibaldi!*

The napoleons amounted to one thousand, which translated into lire came to about six million. Don Camillo could buy old Filotti's house and relocate the altar and the big crucifix in the family chapel, exactly as they were.

He also brought over the Abbot Garibaldi, after having him recovered with stucco by a plaster specialist.

And the first Mass he celebrated in the chapel was for the soul of the departed Alberto Ferrazza. He celebrated it in Latin, of course, in the presence of a few old diehards.

'Lord,' he afterwards explained to the Christ, 'they're a bunch of broken-down old donkeys. They only keep a hold on life because of the strength of their memories of the past and their dear departed. They don't understand that even the Church has to renew itself.'

'Exactly what you don't understand, Don Camillo,' the Christ pointed out.

'Perhaps so, Sir,' Don Camillo admitted humbly. 'In any case, I'm not out of line because this is a private Mass inasmuch as this chapel is now my property, thanks to the help of God!'

'Thanks to the help of Garibaldi,' the Christ amended.

'Lord, it was you who told me to look for the gold where I would find it and precisely there it was that I looked. It's St Antony who compromised my good faith by messing about in the Garibaldi affair.'

'Certainly, Don Camillo,' the Christ said, smiling. 'In a town like this, where the dead people are even more insane than the living, a parish priest like you is just what's called for.'

Naturally it wasn't long before Peppone's spy network informed him about Don Camillo's stroke of good luck.

23

So, coming across Don Camillo in the street one day, Peppone asked with heavy sarcasm: 'Father, is it true you've opened up your own business?'

'No, Comrade. I still work for the same boss. Up there, Mao hasn't yet arrived to disseminate confusion.'

Peppone let it go at that.

Mao does not take to the
water of the Po river

OF the eight parts of the commune administered by
Peppone and his comrades, the one called La Rocca was
the most uncivilized. Only a few miles separated it from
the big town; but not all miles are the same because
not all men are the same, and sometimes, even in a huge
metropolis, all you have to do is turn a corner into a
side street and you find yourself in another world. La
Rocca was situated in the lowlands of the Po, and the
centuries-long fight against the great river had made its
inhabitants hard and violent. To them, anybody who
came from anywhere other than the banks of the Po
river was a foreigner.

Practically all of them were Communists but their
Communism was Stalinism, and the only form of coexistence they recognized involved beating their adver-
saries over the head with a stick.

Doctor Bognoni, therefore, did not encounter much
resistance in persuading the people of La Rocca to found
their own autonomous Maoist cell and name him their
chief. And the day an inspector from the regional
commune arrived in La Rocca to bring the strayed
comrades back to the fold, he found the town walls

papered with Stalinist and Maoist sayings and mani
festos. There wasn't a soul to be found anywhere.

It was inevitable that somebody should take advantage
of the situation and drag out Mao's feat of three years
past. At seventy years of age, Mao had swum fifteen
kilometres at a furious pace; huge yellow posters reminding the people of his triumph were hung on the walls in
Don Camillo's parish and in La Rocca:

Mao astonished the world with his exhibition of strength three
years ago. The time has come for the Maoist comrades of
La Rocca to think over the fact that it appears that their
chief, Comrade Bognoni, cannot himself swim. If its chiefs
cannot swim, how can the proletarian revolution succeed?
Concerned Comrades Who Can Swim

The poster was anonymous but any fool could guess
that Peppone had masterminded it. The La Rocca faction took offence immediately and with typical
impetuousness they counter-attacked with this manifesto:

While the chief of the La Rocca Maoist cell has no pretensions
to being able to swim as well as the great Chairman Mao, it is
certain that he will triumph over the chief of the so-called
'Comrades Who Can Swim'. (Provided, of course, that the fat
accumulated during his career as a petit-bourgeois shop owner
will permit him to remain afloat.)

The reply came immediately:

Attention Little Mao of La Rocca! If after your cod liver oil
cure you feel as strong as a whale, take care you do not end up
as a load of blubber!

The air was warming up and the people became more
and more amused. Naturally when Don Camillo ran
into Peppone and his high command on the street, he
didn't forget to ask cheerfully how training was pro-
gressing and if they had set the date yet for the historic
meet.

'I, stoop to that sort of tomfoolery? Never!' Peppone
retorted brusquely.

'I see,' Don Camillo said, with a hint of malice, 'now that the situation has got out of hand, Mr Mayor, you are contemplating a strategic retreat.'

'Retreat? Never!' Peppone shouted.

'Hooray for our chief!' the high command cheered. 'Priests may have a face for every occasion, but we show the same face to all!'

The match of the century was held one Sunday afternoon and half the world was present on both banks of the river.

The course was across the river and back. A committee was set up on the opposite bank to check the two champions as they finished the first lap; then back to the starting point, with the man who reached it first, of course, being the winner.

Comrade Bognoni was young and thin whereas Peppone, although he was stronger, was longer in the tooth and fatter in the gut. The first lap – the trip out – sent the La Rocca faction into frenzied cheers because Bognoni touched the opposite bank first. But it was those cheers that turned Peppone into a maddened beast and he forgot his years and fat and called up strength he did not know he had for the return trip. Coming back, he caught up with Bognoni, and after a desperate struggle managed to beat him. Peppone touched the finishing line with glorious unconcern, waved debonairly to the cheering crowd, then passed out as cold as a dead fish.

'A doctor, somebody get a doctor!' Brusco shouted, and Peppone's high command, being near at hand, took up the cry.

Peppone did not show any signs of life and Doctor Bognoni, who as usual had brought his little black bag along in case of emergency, was there in a twinkling. He knelt next to Peppone, felt his pulse and shouted to his wife: 'Quick! Prepare a syringe of adrenalin. This man is close to death!'

Bognoni's shouts brought Peppone back to himself. He weakly batted his eyelashes, eyed the doctor with disgust and roared for Brusco. 'Comrade! Remove this charlatan! Can't a man die in peace?'

Bognoni stood up and walked off; then Don Camillo came to kneel by Peppone's side. When Peppone saw him he said, 'Now finally you must be happy.'

'Why on earth should I be happy?' exclaimed Don Camillo.

'Because you are the troublemaker who printed up all those posters that everybody thought I wrote; and you're responsible for this whole filthy mess!'

'I'm afraid so,' Don Camillo admitted humbly. 'But it's a little late now for me to apologize. Can I do anything to help you?'

'Yes,' Peppone roared, 'you can go to hell, you and all the other priests in the universe!'

'Too many people, Comrade. I don't like tour groups,' Don Camillo answered.

Bigio came up with a bottle of cognac and Peppone attacked it as if he were draining the Pontine Marshes.

Then the county doctor arrived and listened to Peppone's heart and measured his blood pressure.

'Perfectly normal,' he said.

'So why has he closed his eyes and become as stiff as a corpse?' Don Camillo asked, worried.

'Because he's stinking drunk, that's why,' the doctor explained.

Peppone was quite drunk, but not stinking. He found the strength to roll over and gurgle: 'Reverend Father, if there's a God in heaven, he'll punish you.'

There is a God in heaven and ordinarily He takes His time. But on this occasion He changed His ways and punished Don Camillo a mere twenty-four hours later.

Hell's angel

ON Monday afternoon Don Camillo was holding a conference with his young assistant in his study, when suddenly in the street, in front of the gate to the courtyard, there exploded a deafening row. A group of seven dishevelled young motorcyclists with bushy manes and leather jackets was gathered at the gate; they were creating an unbelievable din and furiously revving up their motors. Then one of the longhairs took up a strange-looking guitar and all seven began to chant a song (if it could be called that) that would put kinks in a cat's fur, keeping time on their claxons during the refrain.

From the pitch of the voice it appeared that one of the seven was a girl, and coming from her coral lips the lyrics of the song seemed to Don Camillo even more trite.

His bad impression grew worse when the young Hell's Angel doffed her leather jacket and revealed herself to be wearing what amounted to a sleeveless, low-necked blouse in the sweetest pastel flower print that barely covered her bottom.

'I'm going to put an end to this right now!' Don Camillo bellowed, marching resolutely to the door. But the little priest cut him off.

'No, Don Camillo. Let me do it. I know how to handle these young people. Don't pay any attention to their nonconformism; they're actually much finer people than you think.'

Don Camillo went to the window and saw the little priest emerge from the gate and speak smilingly and cordially to the Hell's Angels, who after all weren't that much younger than he. They let him go on for a few minutes, then the girl put her fingers in her mouth and emitted a piercing whistle. The six toughs jumped off their motorcycles and fell upon the little priest, inundating him with a flood of fists and boots.

The little priest was plainly offensive with his pompous speeches and the ridiculous tight-fitting priest-cum-business suit, which Don Camillo could not persuade him to abandon. But the horrible spectacle forced Don Camillo to forget his petty grievances, and like lightning he tore into the pile of Hell's Angels; digging through them he managed to excavate the little priest, who already had been reduced to a ragbag.

The flashy intervention by a priest so big and black threw the longhairs off guard. They stood around looking puzzled for a moment, until the imperious, shrill voice of the girl stirred them into action.

'Get that fat father!' she cried.

The six hooligans pulled themselves together and piled on top of Don Camillo. Their attack was well planned: four of them blocked Don Camillo's arms and legs, and the other two rained blows all over him.

Don Camillo, a passable pugilist under ordinary circumstances, did not expect such an attack and acted like an elephant beset by a tribe of petulant monkeys. It was all he could manage to try and shake the howling rabble off his back. Then came the angry, pouting voice of the girl: 'Come on! Strip off that burlap sack! Let's see what colour longjohns he wears!'

This turned out to be a tactical error for when Don Camillo heard it, he called for the Christ: 'Lord, are you going to allow a minister of God to be stripped down to his underwear in public?'

'Certainly not, Don Camillo,' the distant voice of the Christ replied.

Don Camillo suddenly thought of the race-horse who decides in the last stretch to come out of seventh place and make for the post. Freeing his arms in one swipe, he caught hold of the two toughs tackling his feet, and, gripping their manes, belted the two melonheads against each other. His victims flopped into the dirt at his feet. The other four hoodlums, urged on by the girl, attacked with admirable vigour; unfortunately for them, there happened to be a pole propped up against the gate, a supple, strong acacia stock that in the hands of Don Camillo became a lethal weapon.

They didn't put up much of a fight under this kind of attack and as soon as they could, the Hell's Angels, full of bruises and welts as big as plums, hopped on their motorcycles and took off, shouting over their shoulders, 'We'll see you later.'

Not all seven Hell's Angels, however. The hellish girl stayed behind, leaning against the gate, imperturbably puffing on a cigarette.

Don Camillo was now enflamed, and he started menacingly toward the troublemaker, planning on making her see the light.

The girl didn't bat an eyelash and when Don Camillo was within arm's length she said, smiling, 'Hi, Unc!'

Don Camillo stopped dead and eyed the scantily dressed girl. Decently clothed she would have been a pretty girl, between sixteen and eighteen years old, but her impertinent red locks, her insolent clear eyes, and her immodest mini-skirt made her thoroughly repellent.

'Who do you think you are, Miss Minimonster? What kind of house of ill repute spawned you?'

'I come from your sister Josephine's; in fact, I'm your niece Flora.'

31

'I don't have any niece called Flora!' Don Camillo shouted.

'The truth is, I was baptized Elizabetta,' the semi-clothed girl explained with an angelic smile that could provoke a parish priest to slap her face. 'But the boys call me Flora, for reasons which will become obvious.'

Don Camillo had detected familiar features in that saucy face, and his anger was mounting. 'And you mean to say that you who are supposed to be my niece, the daughter of my only sister, you wanted those long-haired tough friends of yours to beat me up and strip me down to my underwear!' he bellowed.

'Well, one good turn deserves another, Uncle. Wasn't it you who only last week told my mother not to worry about me because you were sure you could swiftly turn me into the sweetest, humblest Daughter of Mary imaginable, right? A regular pillar of the Altar Guild, right? Well, do you still think you can, or would you like me to hop on my bike and scoot back to the big city to console my poor, put-upon old woman?'

Don Camillo gripped the acacia club, but the mini-skirted hellcat continued to hold his gaze defiantly.

'Anselma!' Don Camillo shouted.

Anselma was the bell-ringer's wife. Perhaps it would be more accurate to say, the bell-ringer's husband, since she was one of those women who look like armoured cars; and when they deal out a slap, their victims often can't even remember their own names.

'I cannot touch her,' Don Camillo explained to Anselma when she came out.

'Well, I can,' the armoured car answered; she had been watching the entire episode from the window.

The minigirl didn't seem to care. 'If you dare put your filthy hands on me, I won't answer for what might happen,' she announced, fire in her eyes.

'Don't worry, child,' Anselma reassured her. 'No hands. I leave manual labour to the grape pickers. A dough paddle does the job much more efficiently.'

'Very clever,' Don Camillo said. 'I think perhaps that's the only way to show her the ways of the real world.'

The girl made a strong effort to get away, but Anselma didn't budge an inch.

'Her name is Anselma,' Don Camillo explained to Flora. 'Though everybody calls her "El". It's a nickname for "Elephant". I think you'd better start off by lengthening your skirts about a foot and a half.'

'Never!' Flora squealed with rage.

'Too bad,' Don Camillo sighed. 'That means we'll have to shorten your legs by a foot and a half.'

A wakeful night

FLORA did turn out to be a genuine God-given punishment. Don Camillo quickly found out why his sister, an invalid widow, had given up on the project of straightening out the girl, who'd definitely got off to a bad start.

Flora, the very night of her arrival, laid her cards on the table as far as Anselma was concerned. 'It's not going to do you any good to bar the doors and windows and treat me like a prisoner. I haven't the slightest intention of trying to escape. I want the old bag of a priest to get down on his knees and beg me to leave.'

'Little girl,' Anselma admonished her, 'you don't know what you're saying. Remember that when things were really rough, your uncle confronted bands of Communists that were running amok.'

'Communists, pooh,' Flora sneered. 'Buffoons like the priests, the Fascists, the Liberals, the Socialists, the middle class, the military, the police, the entire Establishment. They're all walking cadavers. Members of the Living Dead. Zombies. We kids are really in control now and nobody's going to stop us from going on!'

'Not even God?'

'*God?*' Flora hooted. 'God is dead.'

Anselma, being the bell-ringer's wife, considered herself dependent on God for her livelihood. She lost her temper. 'If you were my daughter,' she said through clenched teeth, 'I'd give you a slap in the face. But seeing as you're not, I'm going to give you two!' But like certain kinds of explosive, the sound came after the damage was done: by the time she said the word 'two', both slaps had already arrived at their destination.

'They'll help you to sleep,' Anselma explained.

'Well, they'll keep *you* up all night,' Flora said under her breath, as she climbed the stairs to her room.

Flora was prophetic. At two in the morning, the bells began to ring furiously and the entire town was on its feet and running. Don Camillo, too, bounded out of bed, and as soon as he reached the ground floor he ran into Anselma, who was the picture of humiliation.

'What the hell is going on here?' Don Camillo bellowed.

Anselma shook her head in desolation. 'Father, the window of the sun room opens out on the rectory roof, and from the rectory roof a certain troublemaker, who shall remain nameless, can climb out on the church roof and slip in through the little round window in the bell tower . . .'

'And so?'

'Well, since your niece happens to be the troublemaker – I said I wasn't going to mention any names, but you'll find out soon enough that it's her up there, having more fun than a pig at a picnic. And she's pulled the ladders up after her and blocked off the trap-doors at the landings!'

A number of townspeople had gathered and Peppone came up to Don Camillo. 'Father, either you stop this scandal, or I will take the necessary measures!'

'Do take them, then, Comrade Mayor,' Don Camillo answered. 'If you've got a helicopter, get it out and go to work!'

35

Flora had thrown herself into her task with gusto; and now, having discovered the mechanism that operated the carillon, she was composing a pop song on it, with the bells acting as accompaniment for her own inhuman yowls. Hearing her squeals, Smilzo let out a snigger. 'That must be our parish priest's new lady love, calling for her tea!'

Don Camillo would not put up with that sort of joke and picked up Smilzo by his lapels. Peppone intervened. 'You're not going to deny that those are the dulcet tones of a lady?'

'They're the roars of a tiger!' Don Camillo shouted. 'What sin have I committed to deserve this female cyclone, all of a sudden?'

Brusco interrupted him. 'Aha, Father, then the problem is that lively little niece of yours who arrived yesterday with that herd of boyfriends who wanted to reduce you to your underwear.'

Peppone and his pals had a good laugh while in the background Flora's efforts grew louder and louder.

'Lord in heaven,' Don Camillo whimpered, 'how can I make her stop?'

The good Lord took mercy on him. The bell-ringer came over and told Don Camillo in a whisper that there was someone waiting for him in the sun room.

Actually there was some *thing* awaiting him there, a monstrous man straight out of the comic book romances. Jet-black overalls, gloves and crash helmet, the visor pulled down over his face, leaving only his eyes uncovered, he looked like something out of *Diabolique*.

'Father,' the spectre said, 'I think I can help.'

'Venom!' Don Camillo exclaimed. 'What's happened to you?'

'I have to be able to fade into the night,' the youth explained. 'I don't want any of them to see me shaved down to nothing.'

'What about the Army?'

36

'I passed the physical,' Venom answered. 'I'm off with the next shipment of recruits.'

'She's dragged all the ladders up to the belfry and blocked all the trap-doors,' Don Camillo said, turning to the problem in hand. 'How am I ever going to get up there?'

'If there's a lightning rod conductor going up there, I can climb it.'

'No, that's much too dangerous.'

Venom laughed. 'Dangerous for a priest, but not for me.'

He slipped out of the little window over the rectory roof, clambered up to the church roof and grabbed on to the lightning rod wire. Then the night enveloped him.

'Oh, Lord,' Don Camillo moaned, falling to his knees, 'please help him!'

'Don Camillo,' the far-off voice of Christ replied. 'Am I wrong, or didn't you tell me that boy doesn't belong to your flock?'

'No, my Lord, you're not wrong, I'm the one that was wrong. But for the love of God, please don't get distracted! Keep your hand on his brow now!'

'And if he falls, how am I supposed to save him, pull him up by his hair? Especially now that you've shaved him bald?'

Don Camillo began to sweat blood and meanwhile the infernal clanging went on.

Then, suddenly, it stopped.

Don Camillo sped down to the room at the foot of the bell tower. A scrabbling sound could be heard up in the tower. The trap-doors in the landings came open one by one and the ladders dropped down from them. Finally the last trap-door opened, the ladder came down, then Venom appeared, a bundle over his shoulder.

The bundle was Flora.

In order to handle her more easily, Venom had packed her up, using the rope from one of the bells. He'd shut her up by stuffing one of his leather gloves in her mouth.

When they landed on solid ground, Venom held the

37

bundle out to Don Camillo, but the priest drew back his hands and snarled, 'Throw her over in that corner!' Then he shouted for Anselma and she came running.

'Take that foul mess away!' Don Camillo roared, pointing to the girl. 'And tell that mob the show is over and they can go home to bed.'

Evicting Flora from the belfry had been quite a job and Venom was glad to toss down a couple of glasses of wine. They were alone in Don Camillo's study, and Venom had taken off his helmet to let a little air circulate around his shiny round head.

Don Camillo had wanted to be told the details of the enterprise, but Venom shook his head. 'Father, let's forget it and talk about serious things. You've brought the plague into your house. I know her, she's really vermin!'

'Where did you meet her?'

'At Castelletto, two months ago. She was with the Scorpions, a gang of Hell's Angels from the city. They'd come down to Castelletto to start a punch-up, but since Castelletto is our territory, we beat them up and they had to scarper with their heads all bashed in. The six that brought the chick over yesterday are the ringleaders, and since you made them look pretty bad, they're not going to let you off easy. They'll be back.'

'That's fine with me,' Don Camillo growled. 'I've still got a few acacia stocks stashed away in the woodshed.'

Venom shook his head. 'I've got a stoolie in the city and he phoned me to say that the Scorpions have got a big operation planned. The whole flock of them is coming here to shake things up and break the girl out of here.'

'So let them come,' Don Camillo snarled. 'We'll get the police all ready for them.'

'Father, there isn't anything you can do. These boys come when nobody's expecting them. There's about fifty of them and they work together like a machine. They know the fuzz won't shoot at them and they'll get off clean.'

38

Venom was bubbling with rage and stamping up and down the carpet like an angry lion. 'Now why?' he shouted, finally stopping in front of Don Camillo. 'What made you shave my head?'

'What has your hair to do with those hoodlums?'

'A lot, because if I still had my hair I could get up my gang and take care of those Scorpions easy as anything! One of these days it'll sink in with you old relics that we young people, drops-outs, longhairs, rebels, hippies, whatever you want to call us, we have a system all our own and on our own we can take care of things without making tragedies out of them. Oh, God, if only I still had my hair!'

'Hair, schmair,' Don Camillo laughed.

'Look, I can't present myself with my hair like this, it's that simple. It's the bit about losing face.'

'A man is the same no matter what length his hair is.'

'Father, it's easy for me to say to you that a priest is a priest no matter what he's wearing. But it's not so easy for you to try and say Mass in your underwear, right?'

'Don't be silly!'

'Well, it's silly to you now, but yesterday when the vermin tried to strip you down to your underwear, you really made them sweat it out.'

'Never mind,' Don Camillo interrupted. 'It's better this way, we won't have a war between your two gangs.'

'Yes, but how are you going to keep some poor joker from defending himself from the Scorpions by dragging out his shotgun and shooting? Listen, Father, if a boxer runs up against a stranger, if this guy is armed, he's going to defend himself by shooting, and the boxer falls down dead. But if two boxers bump into each other and try to beat each other up, it's only a boxing match and nobody dies. The moral of the story is . . .'

Don Camillo was tired or arguing. He grubbed around in one of the desk drawers and drew out an envelope, which he handed to Venom.

'Milan,' he said, 'isn't far away. And in Milan you can

find anything. Samson was destroyed by Delilah simply because he couldn't make it to Milan. You, however, are free to go there.'

It was three twenty in the morning when Michele Bottazzi, called Venom, exclaimed 'O.K.!', pulled on his helmet, went out and disappeared into the night.

Flora was confined to quarters for two days. Towards six in the evening on Thursday, Anselma let her out in the courtyard where Don Camillo, stretched out in a chaise, was enjoying a bit of fresh air.

The little criminal no longer wore a miniskirt; instead, she was hidden under a mountain of a black dress with a neckline that appeared to creep up over her chin, a hemline that dragged through the dust, and sleeves that hung down six inches past the tips of her fingers. A little black lace handkerchief was pinned to her hair. She had whitened her face with flour and taken off all her other make-up. She looked like an allegory of the Depression.

'Does this suit you, Uncle?' she asked insolently, as she lit a cigarette.

'No,' Don Camillo said placidly. 'The cigarette's out of keeping. A type like you should be smoking Tuscan cigars. Just the same, sit down.'

Flora wanted the people passing by on the street to see her reduced to such austerity, so she preferred to remain standing. But the people who passed by on the street and saw her just sniggered.

Everybody was thoroughly aware of the incident of the girl in the bell tower. For one thing, the previous night at the commune meeting, Peppone, after reminding his constituency that Busseto had footed the bill for Verdi's musical studies, suggested that perhaps the commune should offer to finance the studies of the parish priest's young niece, who had shown such musical talent in the execution of her nocturne a few evenings before.

So it was that people walked back and forth in front of the gate to Don Camillo's little garden-courtyard and sniggered. Suddenly, however, everybody stopped to listen to some powerful motors rumbling in the distance.

It wasn't long before six Hell's Angels paraded past on their motorcycles, slowly, so that everybody could get a good look at their black leather jackets. Then, isolated at a proper distance behind his advance guard, astride his big black Harley, came their chief, his chest proudly puffed out, filling almost to bursting point a black jerkin with a white skull on the back and the word 'Venom'.

His eyes were flashing, and his long, shiny, soft hair wafted in the breeze. Venom was majestic, monumental. When Flora saw him, she covered her eyes. 'That rat!' she cried, full of hate and fury. 'I'm going to make him pay for Castelletto and that episode the other night!'

'Dear child,' Don Camillo advised her with a smile, 'try to stay away from him. He's a violent man and he wouldn't stop short of making you drink an entire bottle of cod liver oil.'

'You underestimate me!' Flora answered, furious. 'You don't know yet what it is to tangle with the Scorpions. I'm going to pull out his greasy hair lock by lock, root by root! I want to hear him squeal with pain! I want to get him really riled!'

'It's not going to be easy,' Don Camillo chuckled, happy, though not overjoyed for he kept thinking about how much Venom's wig had cost.

Flora lost her composure and turned her back on Don Camillo. She walked resolutely toward the gate to the bell tower courtyard. But she forgot that she had on a dress with a hem that dragged in the dust, and it caught in the hortensia branches, sending her headlong into the flower bed.

'The love of flowers is a sign of gentleness of soul,' Don Camillo observed in a loud voice.

One occasion on which a cellar was more important than a dome

DON CAMILLO was having a bad spell. As if Flora wasn't trouble enough, the little priest sent by the Curia was souring his life with his mania for reform. It was logical, therefore, for Don Camillo to pass most of the day in his manor house, newly won with the help of God and, in a certain sense, Garibaldi.

In his new chapel, he had set up the old altar with its huge crucifix, the Abbot St Antony, and all the other trinkets cast out of the parish church by Don Francesco's reformist zeal. The only thing that interested Don Camillo was the chapel, but this was attached to the manor house, and though the walls were thick and solid, the roof was quite decrepit. Therefore, when he wasn't inside the chapel talking to the Christ, Don Camillo was up on the roof, fixing tiles and plugging holes.

It was for this reason that one afternoon he was able to spot a small van pulling up in front of the rusty gate to the nettle-infested garden. Out came Peppone, Brusco and Smilzo, obviously not expecting to find Don Camillo there.

The first to detect the priest's presence was Smilzo, who gave the alarm by shouting to Peppone: 'Hey, chief, what's that big black bird perched on the roof over there?'

'Just a black crow, a species, fortunately, that's becoming extinct,' Peppone answered as loud as he could, as soon as he had registered Don Camillo's presence.

A tile dropped from the sky and grazing his shoulder, shattered at his feet, startling Peppone. 'Hey, Father!' he shouted. 'What kind of joke is that?'

'Oh, forgive me, Comrade Mayor,' Don Camillo shouted from the rooftop. 'I mistook you for that murderer Garrotte. It's a bit of a bother, all you comrades looking alike.'

This was really ungenerous behaviour on the part of Don Camillo, for there wasn't the faintest resemblance, exterior or interior, between Comrade Giuseppe Botazzi, nicknamed Peppone, and Comrade Egisto Smorgagnino, nicknamed Garrotte.

This Garrotte had come back to town at the end of the war and been hailed as a hero; and he had become virtually the spiritual leader of all the Valley's Communists because of his heroic feats as a fighter in the Resistance.

Then in 1947, his record was adjudged severely less heroic, and Garrotte, who had gained his kudos from the enormous quantity of people he had killed, had been sentenced to life imprisonment for murder. Garrotte had taken to his heels to hide behind the Iron Curtain. Twenty years later, Garrotte had been amnestied without having spent so much as one minute in gaol and had returned to the town fat as a pig and arrogant as a cock.

This situation was not to the liking of Peppone or his comrades, and when a big shot from Party headquarters told Peppone that on a certain day Garrotte would be arriving in town and that a suitably festive reception was to be organized and an equally suitable cordon of projection arranged for him, Peppone had answered: 'Right: I'll tell the cops to keep an eye out to prevent him from killing any more people.'

Perceiving how things were, the Party big shot did not insist. However, on the day Garrotte was supposed to arrive, all the walls of the town were papered with posters praising and welcoming the returned hero. And Garrotte's float was followed by an endless queue of cars filled with people flying red banners. There was even a lorry with a brass band on it playing *The Red Flag* and *Bye Bye Baby*.

But Peppone had had nothing to do with it: it was entirely the work of the Bognoni couple and the Maoists from La Rocca. The parade had filed through the deserted streets and stopped in the middle of the square. Here the Bognoni couple climbed on to the Garrotte's float and proceeded to deliver sonorous discourses and eulogies welcoming the brave Comrade who was bringing the spirit of the proletarian revolution back to the Valley. They didn't forget to snipe at 'capitalist' comrades who had turned to 'shopkeeping'.

Peppone and his high command were listening from the waiting room in the town hall, and at this point he commanded: 'Gigiola, let's go!'

Gigiola, the chief of police, had been a whip during the Resistance and had never forgotten it. He moved into the square followed by four cops and began to tuck parking tickets under the windshield wipers of all the cars in the parade, which were lined up in a 'No Parking' zone. Beginning, of course, with Garrotte's car.

From the heights of the truck, Garrotte saw him, jumped down and confronted him menacingly.

'Comrade Gigiola!' he shouted. 'Don't you recognize me?'

'When I'm doing a job, I don't recognize anybody,' the police chief replied. 'The fine is a thousand lire. This is a "No Parking" zone.'

Garrotte, oozing resentment from all his pores, paid up

and said: 'I'll move my car to a place where parking is forbidden to bourgeois comrades!'

That he did, followed by the entire Maoist contingent: he had moved to La Rocca where he had settled in to become the guiding light of the autonomous Maoist cell.

This much is true; however, only the vilest intentions could be behind any assertion that Peppone and Garrotte looked alike. But it annoyed Don Camillo to distraction to see Peppone and his henchmen hovering around his house. What were they up to? What was so entertaining about a priest on a rooftop? They couldn't have 'just dropped by'; to come to the house involved driving up a long private road that ended right in front of the gate of the nettle-infested courtyard. They had obviously come with some evil idea in mind, and the proof was that they were thoroughly disconcerted to find that the house was not deserted.

'Father,' Peppone shouted up, 'aren't you even going to ask us in?'

'I can't possibly receive visitors now,' Don Camillo answered. 'As you see, I have the bricklayers in the house.'

'All I can see is a priest on a roof,' Smilzo sniggered. 'And that's not a pretty sight.'

'If you'll wait a second I'll try and brighten it up with a bit of music,' Don Camillo replied, hoisting up a tile, making as if to throw it at Smilzo's head.

'Now that he's bought himself this dilapidated shanty he doesn't half give himself princely airs!' Smilzo tittered, taking a quick step back.

They clambered into their van chortling like turkeys and drove off.

At sunset, Don Camillo descended from the roof to have a chat with the Christ. 'Lord, what evil scheme brought them over here?'

'Don Camillo, men are not always motivated by evil schemes.'

'Lord, this house has been abandoned for years. Why should they suddenly come round just when the house becomes my property? It's clear they're plotting something against me.'

'Don Camillo,' the Christ reprimanded him, 'why do you give yourself such airs? If the floor here suddenly caved in under your feet, would you believe that a floor built perhaps three hundred years ago had lain in wait for all that time until the precise moment when it could crumble under your feet?'

'Not at all, Sir. In any case there's no risk of that since beneath this pavement is nothing but solid ground.'

To emphasize his declaration, Don Camillo gave the brick paving several hearty stamps, and heard a distant, hollow echo: this was no solid ground down there, but a big hole!

It was ridiculous to think that there was a crypt under a chapel built no more than two hundred years ago as a wing to a manor house. It was more reasonable to think that the cellar underlying the whole house extended beneath the chapel too. Don Camillo collected his torch and went down to inspect the cellar, wherein heaps of ancient junk were rotting silently. Up against the wall that divided the chapel cellar from that of the main house, there was a mountain of barrel staves, and it was next to these that Don Camillo found a square patch of wall which, in spite of the care taken to camouflage it, was clearly of very recent construction. With a piece of roof beam, Don Camillo battered in the wall, which hid a narrow door, and found himself underneath the chapel.

There, diligently oiled and wrapped in grease paper, were ninety machine guns, eighty pistols, and a fair-sized pyramid of small waterproof metal boxes stuffed with ammunition.

Like many manor houses built with a castle in mind, the cellar contained a deep well, long in disuse, but still full of rancid, black water.

It was a tremendous effort, but in a couple of hours, Don Camillo was able to dump all the guns and ammunition into the well, and to top it all off, he threw in an additional pile of debris he had found scattered around the cellar. The black water engulfed everything and covered it over. To work more efficiently, Don Camillo worked in his underwear and tunic; when he had finished the job, he went upstairs, washed, dressed, lay down on an old sofa, and instantly fell fast asleep.

He awoke just after midnight. There were people wandering about inside the house – three people who were talking out loud, certain that there was no one to overhear.

It was inevitable that Don Camillo, who had meticulously polished up one of the machine guns to find out exactly what it was, had forgotten to throw it into the well along with the others: and it was precisely this nasty instrument that the three intruders found aimed at them when Don Camillo, switching on his torch, blocked their passage.

'Well, well,' Don Camillo exclaimed. 'Mr Mayor! To what do I owe the honour of this visit?'

Peppone had no time to answer because other people were arriving too. Not through the front door, unlike Peppone and comrades, but through a first-floor window. They heedlessly tore out the window's iron grille by the roots, causing a rude din. Don Camillo turned off his torch and retreated into a dark corner.

The second shift also numbered three, and these too were talking out loud, very calmly.

'The loot's still in the cellar under the chapel,' one of the three explained. 'I checked the night before last. We've got to get it out in thirty-two minutes because Gino's coming with the tractor and the trailer loaded with tomato crates. It's the tomato season and the roads are jammed with farm trucks taking tomatoes to the factories. When the boy comes, everything must be down there ready to load on the trailer.'

They went into the cellar, but were back in a few minutes, furious.

'Chief,' one of the three said, 'we've been robbed!'

'It could only be Peppone. He was the sole person besides me who knew where the loot was hidden. But I'll make him talk, that sack of . . . Anyhow, we've got to stop the boy from bringing the tractor and tomato-crates!'

'Not at all,' Don Camillo said, lighting the torch and stepping forward while Peppone and comrades backed further into their corner, 'listen to me, Garrotte, let the tomato boy come here. A ride in the fresh air will do him good.'

Garrotte's eyes were fixed on Don Camillo's machine gun.

'Garrottee, see what good care I'm taking of it?' Don Camillo said. 'The same for the rest of it. So go back to La Rocca, and set your mind at ease: when Mao orders you to bring on the proletarian revolution, you have only to come to me to take back your guns.'

Garrotte, gross as a pig, seemed to exude fat and hatred from his person and Don Camillo felt sorry for him.

'You can go now,' Don Camillo said, herding them towards the door.

Garrotte went out into the fresh, starry night, and a powerful kick from Don Camillo aided him to clear the twelve-step stairway easily.

'Your charms lacked only that one touch,' Don Camillo explained. 'Now you may go on your merry way, certain that one day God will cast you into the fires of hell.'

The other two got the same send-off and all three went back to La Rocca with warm backsides. Having dealt with the disreputable trio, Don Camillo returned to make contact with the first onslaught.

'If people find out about this, half the world will split their sides laughing,' Don Camillo explained, but I'm very selfish and want to keep this laugh to myself. Inside of one week the roof must be fixed, Comrade Botazzi!

Comrade Smilzo is quite right: a priest on a rooftop isn't a very pretty sight.'

'You don't imagine *I'm* going to shinny up there on your roof, do you?' Peppone huffed.

'Hardly! Comrade Brusco is a contractor and he can send whoever he feels like up there. The important thing is, Comrade, you're paying for it!'

'This is dirty blackmail!' Peppone protested, trying to put on a ferocious face but not succeeding because, when you come right down to it, things had turned out exactly right.

A thrashing followed by a salting

THE progressive little priest sent by the Curia to straighten out Don Camillo was named Don Francesco, but because of his nervous, wiry frame, his tailored businessman-priest suits, his continual state of agitation, and arrogant attitude, he had been re-named Don Chichi by the entire parish. The name means nothing in itself: it simply captured exactly the way he was.

Don Chichi, having 'demysticized' the church in its externals, was carrying his offensive to the core now, having launched a series of sermons that was a continuous ardent denunciation of the malevolence and guilt of the rich.

A lot of people had stopped coming to Mass and Don Camillo, coming across Pinetti in the street, asked him why he never saw him in church any more.

'I worked honestly all my life for what I have now,' Pinetti answered, 'and it grates to come to church just to be insulted by that Don Chichi.'

'One goes to church out of respect for God, not for the priest. And by staying away from church you show disrespect for God – not for the priest.'

'I know, Father; my brain knows it but my liver doesn't.'

Not a profound pronouncement, but it had a certain logic, and since the defections were increasing, Don Camillo decided the time had come to have a little talk with Don Chichi.

'It is written that "A camel will pass through the eye of a needle more easily than a rich man will pass through the Gates of Heaven",' Don Chichi answered shortly. 'The doors of the Church should be no wider than the Gates of Heaven. God created the earth for all mankind, and a rich man is rich simply because he has taken the share of other men. Were it not for the rich, the poor would not exist, just as the robbed would not exist were there no thieves. The rich man is a thief and property can most accurately be called stolen goods. The Church of Christ is a church for poor folk because the Kingdom of Heaven belongs to the poor alone.'

'Poverty is a disgrace, not a virtue,' Don Camillo answered. 'It's not enough to be poor, to be a just man. And it is not true that only the poor have rights and only the rich have duties. Before God, all men have one thing, their duty to Him. But leaving that aside, you are alienating not just rich people from the Church. Your campaign against war, for example: you're quite right to condemn war but you can't treat people like criminals just because they've fought in a war and perhaps given their health or even their life to it.'

'A man who kills is a murderer!' Don Chichi shouted. 'Just wars and holy wars simply don't exist: all wars are unjust and diabolical! God's commandment is, "Thou shalt not kill". He also says, "Love thine enemy". Can't you see, Father, this is the hour of truth and the time has come to call bread bread and wine wine!'

'That's a precarious position to put yourself in, here where bread and wine are the body and blood of Christ!' Don Camillo roared pigheadedly.

Don Chichi gave him a pitying look. 'Don Camillo, the

Church is a great ship which for many centuries has been tied to the dock. The time has come to weigh anchor and set sail for the high seas! And the time has come to renovate the ship's trimmings too. The time has come for dialogue, Father!'

Don Camillo shrugged his shoulders. 'Twenty years ago, when you were babbling your first word, I was already having it out with the Communists.'

'I am not being facetious, I'm not talking about intransigence and violence!' Don Chichi shouted. 'I mean dialogue, true coexistence.'

'Argument is the only possible sort of dialogue with Communists,' Don Camillo answered. 'After twenty years of quarrels, here we all are, still alive: I cannot picture any better way of coexisting than this. The Communists bring me their children to be baptized and they get married before the altar, while I, for my part, bestow on them as I do to non-Communists only the right to obey God's laws. My church is not the great vessel you are talking about but only a poor little boat: but it has always been able to go from one shore to another. Now you are at the helm and I let you take it where you want because I have been ordered to do so: however, I do advise you not to capsize my boat. You alienate many men from the old trimmings so as to take on newcomers from the other shore: watch out that you don't lose the old without finding the new to replace them. Remember the story of the two friars who threw the tiny shrivelled peaches they had into the dirt, assuming they would later find beautiful ripe ones on the trees beyond – those trees had no peaches at all and the two friars had to return to their old peaches, only to find them eaten by worms.'

'How your stories of the two friars do come in handy!' said Don Chichi, laughing. 'The good sower does not throw his seed on to the field until he has cleared it of weeds.'

Don Camillo was a poor country priest and, unlike Don Chichi, had read few books and did not even read many newspapers. So, apart from the changes in liturgy, he had no idea what this new direction the Church was supposed to be going in was all about. Nor could he understand it, because before everybody else, in fact twenty years before them, Don Camillo had already been going in the same new direction and doing just that had got him into some fearsome fixes. It stood to reason, then, that he wasn't going to sympathize with the cub priest who, having arrived to teach Don Camillo how to be a priest, had in fact done nothing but empty out his church.

Sic stantibus rebus (that is, at this juncture) Pinetti came into the rectory.

'My daughter is getting married,' Pinetti said. 'But I want her to get married the same way me and my wife were and my father and mother before us: in front of the same altar with the same Mass said.'

'Your daughter will be married as the Church has decreed!' Don Chichi countered aggressively. 'Keep in mind, Mister Pinetti, that this is not a shop where one can choose the merchandise one prefers. And, particularly, remember that before God, your money isn't worth dirt!'

'It's worth considerably more than that to my daughter and her fiancé,' Pinetti snapped. 'So if those two want me to shell out her dowry, they'd better get the Mayor to marry them!'

Don Chichi jumped to his feet. 'If this is your kind of Christianity,' he shouted, 'it's no great tragedy for the Church to lose a Christian like you!'

'Just as it's no great blessing to the Church to have priests like you!' Pinetti shouted as he stalked out of the door.

Don Camillo hadn't said a word, but after Pinetti had gone, he sighed. 'That will be the first civil ceremony ever performed in my parish.'

'Is that any reason to give in to that rascal's blackmail?'

'He's not a rascal and he wasn't asking for anything contrary to the laws of God.'

'The Church must renew itself!' the little priest shouted. 'Do you mean to tell me you know absolutely nothing about what went on at the Ecumenical Council?'

'Yes, I've read about it,' Don Camillo answered. 'But it's quite difficult for me. I cannot go much beyond the word of Christ. Christ spoke in a simple, clear way. Christ was not an intellectual, He used no complicated phrases, only the humble, easy words that everybody knows. If Christ had been present at the council, His talks would have sent the erudite conciliar delegates into gales of laughter.'

'You never stop joking,' the little priest answered. 'But you know that if Christ returned to earth today, he would not speak the way people do now.'

'No,' Don Camillo agreed. 'Otherwise the poor ignorant folk like me would not understand him.'

'Don Camillo, the truth is, you don't *want* to understand!'

'I only know the facts. And to me, the fact of Pinetti's daughter's civil ceremony is much more important than all the erudite conciliar delegates' erudite conciliar dialogues put together. A civil ceremony is an embarrassment to the Church and an insult to God. Precisely that, particularly when the real problem is that the Church, in suddenly opening its doors, suddenly discovers a world where the majority of the people don't believe in God. Millions of people no longer have any religious faith at all. This is the only thing I understood out of everything that was said at the council. And it is the most important thing of all.'

Don Chichi spread his arms in despair. 'Without blowing the incident out of proportion,' he said, 'I agree that it would be better if that civil ceremony were not performed. Why don't you marry them in your little chapel? It's a private chapel and the old ceremony would be allowable there.'

'I will give it the most serious thought,' Don Camillo answered.

Actually he didn't give it a second thought because it was precisely what he had dreamed of all along. Pinetti's daughter was indeed married in Don Camillo's chapel, and there were so many people present that they filled not only the chapel but the garden outside too. And among the guests were all those people that Don Chichi had alienated from the church and this was a great consolation to Don Camillo, a consolation that he had deep need of, because every day his horrendous niece made his life more bitter.

Flora was his niece's nickname, and if there was ever on this earth a young girl less like a flower, Don Camillo could not imagine such a creature. It seemed as if there could be no one on the face of the earth capable of causing one half of the trouble that Don Camillo's niece could produce.

Although Anselma had clear ideas and heavy hands, and didn't bat an eyelid about spanking Flora whenever the occasion to do so arose, this didn't change things in the slightest.

'I'll get my own back, with interest,' Flora said each time.

Anselma cackled with glee: this she would not have done had she known what the girl was plotting. Venom was not mistaken, and the onslaught began on a boring, sunny, sleepy holiday afternoon.

The town was quiet; in the square, empty chairs and tables at the café were becoming red hot under the sun. Shopkeepers propped up against their doorsteps snoozed on their teetering wicker stools. In the bars and lobbies, the usual old men in silent conversation clutched their glasses of ruby wine.

It was like the great tempest of '68. In a moment the town was turned into an inferno. Thirty Scorpions in black leather jackets rounded the curve into the square, atop thirty thundering motorcycles.

The gang that left the city had numbered fifty but at a

certain point along the way, twenty of them had veered off towards Castelletto, while the rest had taken up a position behind a hedge.

When they reached Castelletto, the twenty had set about smashing everything they could lay their hands on. The chief of police, warned by telephone, took four of the six policemen entrusted to him to guard the entire territory, and scampered over to Castelletto, leaving behind only the deputy and the turnkey. Then the group of thirty Scorpions attacked the defenceless town.

Having dismembered all the tables and chairs in the square riding round on their maniacal carousel, the thirty wild hoodlums jumped off their machines and began to devastate the shops, beating up any poor soul who stood in their way.

At the same time, a select band was closing in on the church via the side streets. Flora, who had organized the entire coup by telephone, ran to the window of the bell-ringer's house as soon as she heard the motors.

'Come inside,' she ordered the toughs. 'Before you get me out of here, you have to help me take care of something.'

Anselma slept on the first floor and, luckily, had locked her door with a chain. There were four Scorpions, though, and the chain could hardly withstand their rabid charge. Flora was the first one in: she picked up the dough paddle and, pointing at Anselma who was trying to pull something over her shoulders, ordered: 'Hold her tight while I settle our account.'

Anselma fought like a lioness but the four boys were soon able to hold her still, face down on the bed. Flora raised the dough paddle. 'When I get through with you, you won't be able to sit down for three years,' she howled. 'And not even that fat priest of yours will be able to fix it up for you.'

Then, everything happened in a second. A hand as big as a spade latched on to her hair while at the same time another took the dough paddle out of her grasp. Venom

56

and eight of his country toughs had come to the rescue. The four Scorpions attacking Anselma were quickly rendered helpless.

It was quite a struggle to stuff the first of the four through the window, but after he had dropped to the pavement below with a thud, the others were a cinch. Old houses in the Valley are small and a flight from the first floor is no traumatic affair. In any case, the four hooligans were hard as rocks and, bouncing on the ground, they only broke a few minor bones.

'Anselma,' Venom said, 'we've got to get moving; do you think you can take care of this snotnose by yourself?'

'Don't worry,' Anselma reassured him. 'I'll roast her for dinner.'

In the square, the Scorpions were resisting the country gang quite efficiently, but the arrival of Venom and the eight additional thugs marked the turning point of the battle. Venom was a practical young man and when it was clear that the Scorpions were near the end, he said to his men: 'If we keep it up, we're going to have to carry them home ourselves. I think it's better if they go home alone. Let's let them go.'

The Scorpions dragged themselves on to their motorcycles and lit out like jets.

The whirlwind intervention of Venom and his gang of country toughs was enough to convince the men of the town, who had improvised an army to repulse the invader, not to get involved in the battle. But they didn't want the Scorpions to leave without some souvenir. The Scorpions rode their motorcycles affecting a rather unusual pose: stomachs flat against their petrol tanks, rears in the air, they looked like jockeys; and, as an afterthought, the townspeople decided to let them have a little taste of buckshot. But the leader of the group of men had a smattering of Latin and said: 'No, friends, no lead. One must act *cum grano salis*.'

And so they loaded their cartridges with grains of salt. Anybody who has felt the pangs of bits of salt in his seat will tell you that he would not rush back to the town that distributed souvenirs of that sort.

The twenty-six city-bred seats, once out of the town, entered the ambush area and were roundly salted up. Only twenty-six because the four Venom and his friends had defenestrated remained, stunned and dazed, in the bell-ringer's vegetable garden. Peppone himself came to arrest them, Smilzo, Brusco and Bigio tagging along to lend a hand; just as they were about to load the four tearaways and their motorcycles on to the back of a lorry for the police to deal with, Don Camillo arrived, having passed the afternoon blissfully puttering around his house hidden in the green. He had no idea of what had been going on.

'Who are these four goons?' asked Don Camillo.

'Visitors from out of town, Father,' Peppone explained. 'Thanks to your dear little niece, we are enjoying a great influx of tourists. She's quite a girl, your niece. You must introduce us one day.'

'She already knows enough troublemaking lunatics,' Don Camillo muttered to himself.

Revenge

THE little priest's aggressiveness continued to depopulate the church, and, just as Don Camillo had foreseen, recruits from the other shore, deaf to all blandishments and solicitations, did not arrive to fill the empty pews.

Nonetheless, in answer to Don Camillo's recriminations, the little priest still did nothing but repeat, 'The good sower clears his field of rank weeds before sowing his seed.'

'The good sower,' Don Camillo amended, 'checks to see whether the soil is arable before he sows his seed.'

'All soil is arable!' the little priest squeaked. 'A thread of water suffices to make the driest desert sand sprout luxuriant vegetation! This was the mistake of the old Church: it divided the world into good and bad. It is precisely in this arid land that the new Church will sow good seed after fertilizing it with its sweat and tears, and even its blood, if necessary! I will bring Christ to the margins of society, to its outcasts, to those rejects forced to beg for a living, to the sinners forced to sell themselves for a living, to the disgraced girls seduced and abandoned by a society who then turns away from them, erecting a wall of contempt around them!'

'Oh, I see,' Don Camillo said. 'You've decided to move to another parish.'

'What's that you say?'

'I mean, you're not likely to find people like that around these parts,' Don Camillo explained. 'If you spot any beggars, they're professionals who come from far away or tramps who come by train for market day. As for lost girls, there are those, just as there are every other place in the world, but they don't do it for a living.'

'You mean to say you don't have any unwed mothers?' Don Chichi asked sarcastically.

'Oh yes, a few.'

'I will bring Christ to those poor outcasts!'

Desolina came in with the post.

'Then you can start right away,' Don Camillo informed the little priest. 'Desolina here is one of those poor outcasts you should be bringing Christ to.'

'Maybe *he's* an outcast, but I wouldn't know anything about it,' Desolina said, pointing to Don Chichi. 'As for Christ, I know where to find him without being led around by this shepherd.'

Don Chichi took offence. 'Is this the way a sinning woman rejected by society speaks to a minister of God? Where is your humility!'

'Maybe your sister's a sinning woman rejected by society,' the lady defended herself sharply. 'When I was sixteen I had a child and I brought him up working honest and hard; then, when he went to start his own family, I helped out with his young ones. Now that the oldest of these has a baby eight months old, I'm raising him too but in spite of that I find some time to help out here at the rectory. The way I see it, I have been quite humble enough throughout my seventy-two years on this earth!'

Desolina stalked out, her head held high in fierce pride, and Don Camillo explained to the priest: 'This is an unusual case of an unwed mother who is also an unwed grandmother and an unwed great-grandmother. However, there are more ordinary cases around. Unfortunately they are all girls who live with their parents and I wouldn't go around stirring up any dust if I were you, because they've all got fathers and brothers who are pretty brutal when it comes to people messing about with their family problems.'

'Would you mind telling me what kind of primitive society I've fallen into?' Don Chichi exploded.

Don Camillo spread his arms helplessly. 'All you can do is pray to the Lord to send you some beggars, lost women, and unwed mothers rejected by society.'

'I am not amused, Reverend,' Don Chichi snapped. 'Dissolution and injustice must exist here just as they do everywhere else, whether or not they are hidden under the dark mantle of hypocrisy!'

'Don't lose hope,' Don Camillo said. 'He who looks shall find.'

Don Chichi looked and found.

There, in the slice of rich land that simmers under the sun, stretching along the right bank of the Po, the peasants have discovered that making bread and pasta at home or taking care of a vegetable garden is a waste of time and so they buy everything, even wine sometimes, at the market. Giosuè was the only one of them who still had a vegetable garden with some fruit trees and two rows of muscatel grapes; and so, his tottering cart towed by a decrepit nag running at half strength, he travelled round to the villages selling vegetables and fruit.

Don Chichi came across him one burning afternoon in the dead of summer, up to his knees in mud, trying to drag his cart back on to the highway, after its right wheel had fallen into the culvert.

Don Chichi got out of his little red Fiat, gave the old man a hand, and then struck up a conversation. 'How old are you, friend?'

'Eighty-seven.'

'And you're still obliged to work for a living?'

'Not at all: I live to keep working.'

Don Chichi was indignant. 'That's appalling! You have the right to rest now!'

'There's no hurry, I'll have a long rest when I die.'

'No, you should retire now. Society's duty is to support you.'

'I'm perfectly capable of supporting myself, boy!'

'Don't call me boy. I'm the assistant priest in this parish!'

'You're a priest? Dressed like that?'

'What's my suit got to do with it?'

'Plenty, just like the Alpine Corps' hats which helped you distinguish them in the war. I know, I fought in the '15–'18 war and I know.'

'That's nonsense, old man! The truth is, society is indebted to you and should pay you.'

'Society has always paid me for anything I've given it. Watch you don't rock my boat, young whippersnapper!' Giosuè said, giving his horse a vicious lash that sent the nag careering down the highway like a thoroughbred.

But Don Chichi was now on his high horse, and there wasn't anything that could stop him. He went straight to the mayor and explained that to let a poor old man of eighty-seven roam round unprotected was an utter disgrace to the community.

'One of these days they'll find the poor duffer dead in a ditch by the river bank, and it will be you who murdered him!'

'Me?' Peppone stammered.

'Not you personally but the community you stand for.'

Don Chichi was a thoroughly articulate young man and he buried Peppone under a mountain of weighty accusations. Finally Peppone said, 'All right, what would you like me to do about it?'

'There's an old people's home in town: make them take him in.'

'Giosuè is a stubborn old soul and I'm sure I don't know how to convince him.'

'Just have the authorities pick him up before it's too late!'

Peppone took the matter under consideration and by chance, several days later, Giosuè was found unconscious on his cart on the river road. Peppone, taking advantage of the situation, had him brought over to the old people's home, which was a villa with a pretty garden, on the outskirts of town.

Don Chichi found out immediately and ran to crow to Don Camillo.

'It's the stupidest thing you could have done,' Don Camillo snapped brusquely.

'But Father, they found him dying.'

'Dying my foot. He simply had too much to drink and the sun knocked him out. This happens every summer. Tomorrow I'm going to take him out of there myself.'

Don Chichi puffed up his skimpy chest. 'I will do everything in my power to stop you, Don Camillo! I will use force, if necessary!'

'The force of public opinion, I imagine,' Don Camillo retorted, 'because if I'm not mistaken there's not much you could do physically.'

Don Camillo did not have the chance to free Giosuè, because the old man freed himself. Having slept off his drink and finding himself in the old people's home, Giosuè – that very night – flew the coop. While scaling the wall round the place, he unfortunately fell from a high spot straight down on his head. But he managed to drag himself as far as the cemetery and there it was that they found him the following morning, stone cold dead in front of a little funerary chapel.

'That's his chapel,' Don Camillo explained to the little priest. 'Giosuè was still working because he wanted to finish it. He used to say, "I want to be buried like a gentleman in my little chapel, alongside my wife – and if I have not finished it, I will not let myself die".'

'That's utter nonsense,' Don Chichi exclaimed. 'We're all the same when we face death. What difference can a grave make? They ought to make a law establishing a

63

uniform kind of grave and funeral. Giosuè was a senile old man caught up in his superstitions. I had him put in there for his own good.'

'Then according to you it's better to die of rage, a prisoner in an old people's home, than to live free and happy, supported by your own efforts?'

'Old people should retire and rest!' the little priest insisted.

'I would say that they also have the right to live,' Don Camillo growled.

A few days went by and Giosuè was not mentioned: the death of an eighty-seven-year-old man does not cause great comment. The crucified Christ was the first to raise the issue again.

'Don Camillo,' He said, 'can't you hear that poor little priest pacing up and down, up and down, every night in his room?'

'No, Sir; at least I pretend not to hear it.'

'Have you been able to trick your conscience?'

'No, Sir, I haven't. But it doesn't seem right to me, this wanting to find wrongs where there are none, this wanting to revolutionize everything!'

'Don Camillo, I too was a revolutionary.'

'Please, there is no comparison!'

'Well then, why are you letting that poor boy suffer on the cross?'

So Don Camillo went to have a talk with the little priest. 'You're looking very poorly and I don't like it,' he said. 'Go to the doctor and get him to prescribe a tranquillizer for you.'

'There's no pill on earth that will keep me from coming face to face with that old man every night. What does he want from me?'

'Probably he wants you to help him finish his chapel.'

Don Chichi had read too many books and he answered, 'Why throw away good money on a dead man who doesn't need anything when there are so many people alive who need so much?'

'Don't tell me about it, tell old Giosuè every night when he comes to haunt you.'

'Giosuè is dead and he won't come to haunt anybody.'

'All right, explain *that* to Giosuè. Tell him to behave like a dead man, then.'

Don Chichi started to laugh; but that night too Don Camillo heard him pace up and down his room far into the night.

One morning, Don Chichi blurted out: 'And how would one find out how the old man wanted his damn chapel finished off?'

'Simple enough,' Don Camillo answered. 'I just happen to have the blueprint. The chapel was a secret between myself and Giosuè. He wanted to surprise everybody. He'd say: "Now when poor penniless Giosuè kicks the bucket, everybody's going to be waiting to see him tossed into some gaping hole in the earth, and won't their jaws drop when they see me carried into this great princely chapel. And then, just because old Giosuè likes company, he's going to have his wife moved over there too!" He got a big kick out of picturing people's faces. When he scraped together a few lire, he'd bring them to me and I'd arrange to have the work done. It will take two hundred and fifty thousand lire to finish the whole thing.'

Don Chichi asserted that it would be the sheerest insanity to throw away that kind of money. Then he sold his little red Fiat and part-exchanged it for a second-hand two-cylinder model. Finally he paid his debt to old Giosuè and he could sleep without being haunted.

Now you will say, 'What a fable!' and 'Superstitious nonsense!' But that's because you have no idea how many stubborn ghosts are buried in the Valley near the great river Po. It is a land unlike any other: flat, even, and within that endless sky above it, there is always room for the dead, while the sky flattens the living below and makes them feel smaller than they really are.

Even Flora, after her violent revolutionary activities,

quietened down. Perhaps it was that endless sky that made her become a girl like any other girl.

Flora had hours when she could come and go, and she never took advantage of them to start trouble. It was obvious that Flora had burned her bridges with the past.

Don Camillo was bursting with delight, and one late afternoon on a roasting August day, when he saw Peppone and his high command cross the churchyard where there was a bit of shade to be had, he cheerfully greeted the mayor: 'Afternoon, Mayor! How are the dear Maoists of La Rocca?'

Peppone and his entourage stopped dead. 'Not so bad, Father,' Peppone answered. 'How about your dear little niece? It's been quite a while since we heard her play.'

'Mayor,' said Don Camillo, 'I promised my sister to transform that girl into a faithful Daughter of Mary and it won't be long now before she is!'

'That's a shame,' Peppone answered. 'A real waste. I'd given the girl credit for a lot more spirit.'

'But, Chief,' Smilzo interrupted, 'how can she help it if she has a priest for an uncle?'

'You have a point,' Peppone admitted. 'Having a priest for an uncle *is* hard luck.'

Don Camillo felt his nose itch. 'Are you saying that you consider it *hard luck* for a brat of her ilk to have an uncle who tears her away from a mob of unruly longhaired ruffian hoods and brings her back into the company of decent people?'

'I didn't make myself clear, Father: what I meant to say is that a girl can behave decently and cordially even without being thrown into a nest of altar-kissing spinsters. I fervently hope I never see the poor girl trailing along in a procession with a candle in her hand.'

'I hate to disappoint you, Mayor, but you'll see just that, very soon, in fact. And what a magnificent sight it will be!'

Peppone just laughed. However, just at that moment a great uproar from the other side of the square reached

66

their ears, and at the intersection where the road led off to the stadium, appeared the head of a long procession.

'What's going on?' Don Camillo exploded. 'The proletarian revolution's broken out?'

'Calm down,' Peppone explained laughing. 'We don't have to make revolutions any more to gain power; we'll take over through elections. It's just the people coming back from the Unity demonstration.'

Meanwhile the procession moved into the square and the brass band leading the way broke into *The Red Flag*.

The entire town had filled the square and was making room for the procession, which was marching towards the churchyard. Behind the band, towed along by a tractor, a farm dray joggled forward, covered with red flags. On top of the dray, a tall pedestal with steps had been built and adorned with red carnation festoons, and at the summit was a golden throne, a girl elegantly draped in a red mantle with train standing propped against it. Her mantle had a devastating slash up her left leg, so that the beautifully shaped limb was completely exposed to view. The little queen wore a sparkling crown surmounted with a hammer and sickle, and across her torso was a sash with the inscription 'Miss Unity'.

While the band went on playing *Bye Bye Baby*, the tractor pulled up to the rectory doorstep. After she saluted the cheering mob with her arm straight, fist clenched, the little queen descended majestically from her throne via a little wooden staircase that the town's youth group had covered with a red carpet and flashily fastened to the dray.

Don Camillo was speechless.

'She's not bad, for a Daughter of Mary,' Peppone commented. He and his high command had remained in spiteful attendance.

'Indeed,' Smilzo put in, 'it must give you great satisfaction as the parish priest to see your young niece receiving so many honours!'

Flora, the picture of impudence, swept off, swaying her

hips like a stripper, in the direction of the rectory, followed by four rather disreputable-looking maids of honour who were carrying her train. As she went past Don Camillo, she raised her clenched fist in salute, smiled radiantly, and sang out: 'Bye-bye, Unc Baby!'

Trapped by Peppone and company, Don Camillo couldn't raise a finger. But so powerful was his determination to kick Flora in the seat of the pants that the girl sensed it without looking at him and leaped out of range. Once inside the bell-ringer's house, she came out on to the little first-floor balcony, saluted with clenched fist before the howling crowd, and threw them flowers and kisses.

Don Camillo was panting and for a moment he thought he'd had a stroke. But then he got hold of himself and said to Peppone: 'Comrade, you have perpetrated an outrage!'

'Not nearly as outrageous as your forcing me into the swimming contest with Bognoni, when I almost had to hang up my skin. In fact, out of this you'll be able to read *Unity* free for a year, because one of the many prizes your niece won is a complimentary subscription.'

'I'll bring it to you myself every morning,' Smilzo added cheerfully. He got away with it only because a look, even one from a frenzied priest, cannot kill.

But she had a heart after all

OF all the bad jokes that Flora had perpetrated, by far the worst was being elected 'Miss Unity', as far as Don Camillo was concerned. It threw him into such a state that the doctor had to give him an injection to calm him down.

He didn't see Flora again until the next afternoon.

'You had no call to do that to me!' he screamed at her, furious. The only reason he didn't tear her apart was because Don Chichi was standing by.

'Why not?' Flora demanded insolently. 'I knew perfectly well it would tick you off, and I'm glad it did!'

Of course Smilzo had deposited the first instalment of *Unity* on the rectory steps that morning, and Don Camillo now hurled it at the girl's feet. 'Look what you've done, hellcat!' he shouted. 'Just think what it will do to your mother and your grandmother Celestina when they see the front page!'

'Don't be idiotic, the gorgon and the troll don't read *Unity*,' Flora retorted while she studied the reproduction of her countenance that embellished the sheet.

'Well, don't worry, somebody is sure to show it to them!'

'So? As if it were a sin to be the queen of a festival. And besides that, it reads rather nicely: "Miss Flora, the lovely niece of Don Camillo, parish priest, was elected Miss Unity etc. etc." and look here, ". . . to her uncle's great joy and satisfaction." There, I was very discreet: I only gave them my professional name and made them promise that all they would do is say I was your adorable niece.'

'They might as well have printed your name anyway!' Don Camillo shouted.

Don Chichi started to laugh. 'Don Camillo, why are you so angry? In fact, this is a bit of comic relief to invigorate the rapprochement between the Church and the Party.'

'Young man!' Don Camillo roared. 'If once I made the blunder of saving you from the clutches of this creature's fellow beasts, you know I can always finish off the job myself! Take yourself and your rapprochement out of this room!'

Don Chichi disappeared before taking another breath, while Flora commented, giggling: 'I think this war between the crow and the cat is awfully funny!'

Don Camillo quickly reminded himself of the Fifth Commandment, which was fortunate, but to distract himself from strangling the dear child he took a walk in the fields, which was unfortunate.

Because, shortly thereafter, a taxi let out in front of the rectory Flora's paternal grandmother, old Celestina, who charged inside to find her granddaughter admiring her picture in the paper.

'Why, oh why did they kill him?' Old Celestina had evidently lost her mind. Ripping the newspaper out of her granddaughter's hands, she snarled furiously: 'You monster, I've always protected you, but this time I simply will not! That's the last straw, getting yourself elected queen of those swine!'

'Those swine or these swine, it's all the same to me,' Flora tittered happily. 'And I don't understand why my dear old granny is getting so hot under the collar. All I wanted to do was give the holy crow a run for his money, and that I certainly did!'

'You certainly did not do anything of the kind; what you did was insult your father!'

'My father?' Flora said, astonished. 'What's he got to do with it?'

'What he has to do with it is that they were the ones who killed him! Not only that, but the man that murdered him is now back here, free and gloating, without having done so much as one day of hard labour. Imagine how funny he must think this picture is, that assassin Garrotte!'

Don Camillo came back from his walk just then and grabbed the old woman by the scruff of the neck to carry her out bodily to the waiting taxi. But it was already too late. When he returned to the rectory, there was the girl, calmly puffing on a cigarette.

'What's got into the old troll?' she asked.

'I think she has already told you what got into her and there's nothing more to add.'

'Why didn't anybody bother to tell me before?'

'Because children should be able to walk towards the future without having to drag behind them the weight of a past that isn't theirs. And because you're a wild one, just like he was. Or, much worse than he was. He would do things first and think about them later. You do things without thinking about them before or after. He was a man who was afraid of nobody and nothing and always said exactly what he thought. In the war, he was a paratrooper and he'd learned not to fear anything.'

Don Camillo spread his arms out in supplication. 'Dear child, let's drop the subject . . .'

'Dear child my foot!' Flora shouted. 'I was born in October, 1949, and in a few months I'm going to be twenty-one. And when I am, I'm really going to open your eyes!'

'I don't see how you can make any bigger messes than

71

you already have. Anyway, in 1949, the air here was pretty foul. The war was over but we still had the civil war going on. Your life, shall we say, was worth about as much as your shoes. People were poisoned with hatred and with politics and the extremists, who had been trained in schools for violence, were making things as bad as they could. The Reds were sure that they could gain power and removed anybody who got in their way. Now, Krik . . .'

'Krik? Who's Krik?' the girl asked.

'Your father. They called him Krik because he was so strong. He was a type like Venom.'

'A stupid wet like that?' Flora interrupted, clenching her fists.

'Venom is neither stupid nor wet. Krik always said exactly what was in his mind, in the square and in the cafés. Even during town meetings, if somebody said something he didn't agree with, he'd jump up and contradict them. So, one night when he was coming home, they shot him in the back with a machine gun. You were only two months old, because it happened in December. Your grandfather and your grandmother Celestina sold their farm and moved to town to help your mother and bring you up. With the fine results that we are here today to observe.'

'And this Garrotte, after bumping off my old man and a whole lot of other people, and after he was supposed to be thrown inside for life, he gets away and now he's legally free and he comes back here a big hero?'

'More or less,' Don Camillo shrugged.

'You and your society nauseate me!' Flora snapped. 'I knew there was something missing from my life!'

'There's something missing from your head!' Don Camillo snapped back.

'No, my very reverend Father Uncle! The hole is inside the heads of hypocritical lying old men like you! If we young people are restless and rebellious, obviously there's some reason for it. We feel that the world out there is a pile of filth filled with vermin and the laws you make serve to disguise this pile of filth and those vermin as moral society and pious citizens. We kids may not have the strength to tear down the whole slimy world, but at least we have the courage to spit on it. In any case, my old man must have been an idiot, because otherwise he wouldn't have let them bump him off.'

'He was an honest man!'

'When you're dealing with vermin, honesty is idiocy.'

'Honesty is always and only honesty. Your father was right.'

'Anybody who gets bumped off is wrong. Always.'

'No!' Don Camillo exploded. 'The justice of the Lord is behind everything.'

'So I hear tell,' the girl drawled. 'However, ever since the miracle went out of fashion, it's been pretty hard to blow the breath back into a dead man's lungs, justice or no justice.'

Don Camillo had been mortally afraid that Celestina's bursting in would upset the girl, but seeing that Flora was accepting the revelation calmly, in fact almost apathetically, even though she was filled with disdain, he thanked God and ended the conversation.

The girl kept up a steady, rhythmic tapping and humming, and after a week, Don Camillo was convinced she had a Beatles record in place of a heart. Then one afternoon, Anselma appeared in the rectory to announce that Flora had broken the lock on the woodshed door and had disappeared with her motorbike.

'Good riddance,' Don Camillo said. 'Undoubtedly she's gone home: better for all concerned.'

'I don't think so,' Anselma answered. 'She left all her things here. Even her record player and her blasted records.'

'Girls of her type, if they had to choose between saving their child or their records, would drop the child into the sea. That means we'll see her back soon. But let's not think about her until she gets back.'

However, he had to think about her before that, because when he went upstairs to his room, he discovered that, although his rifle and his over-and-under shotgun were in their places, his five-shot Browning was nowhere to be found. And his shell case was empty. Suddenly his head felt full of wind, and he said: 'Lord Jesus, please start thinking for me, because I think I've lost the ability!'

Peppone was at home checking over some of the town records with his wife when Don Camillo appeared before him, with an expression on his face that Peppone had never seen before.

'You murderer!' Don Camillo shouted. 'Wasn't it enough to make her Queen of the Unity Festival? Did you have to go and publish the daughter of Krik's picture in your lousy newspaper?'

'Krik's daughter?' Peppone babbled. 'What daughter?'

'Flora!' Don Camillo shouted. 'Flora is Krik's daughter. And Krik's mother saw the picture and came charging down here and blurted out everything to the girl. And now she's gone off on her motorcycle with my Browning!'

Peppone turned white. 'I had no idea,' he sighed. 'You have three sisters, how was I to know that this girl was Krik's daughter? She wouldn't tell me her last name.'

'That's just fine, you didn't know; anyway it doesn't make any difference now: she's just as impetuous as her father and if she brings on some disaster, the whole thing will be on your head!'

'Father, you're jumping to conclusions,' the wife said. 'Perhaps she went out to shoot squirrels.'

'God willing,' Don Camillo said. 'But what if she's gone after Garrotte?'

Peppone jumped up. 'That will be the end, because Garrotte's always got two bodyguards with him and he might end up killing her too. He's going around the area

74

today making propaganda speeches. We must find him and stop him, or at least find the girl!'

Peppone organized the search party. He went off in his big Fiat, Brusco went in his little Fiat, Bigio in the van, and Smilzo on his motorbike.

'We don't know which way Garrotte went, and there are five roads going from La Rocca,' Peppone explained. 'So she's obviously not in town, because that's where he lives. She's probably waiting for him along one of the roads. As soon as we get to La Rocca, we will each take one road. Maria, as soon as Michelone comes home, send him over to La Rocca and tell him to take the main road back.'

'Meanwhile, I'm going ahead,' Don Camillo said. 'I have my bicycle. I'll cross the river where it's dry and take the main road to La Rocca and then come back.'

Flora knew just where Garrotte had gone and which of the five roads he would be using to come back, and so she had taken up a position along the main road, hiding behind a dilapidated wayside shrine that was surrounded by shrubs. The girl had studied her plan carefully and perfected all the details. The new road, at the vantage point she had chosen, had been blasted through a hill; at the top of the embankment was the abandoned wayside shrine, and to one side of the shrine, a poplar. Flora had sawed through the trunk, leaving only a piece of bark on the road side. A cord anchored by the shrine kept the tree upright; all that was required to cause the tree to crash down and stop traffic was to cut the cord. Her motorcycle was hidden in a clump of trees and gorse. She knew what Garrotte's car looked like, his licence number, and she'd memorized all the features of his face.

'You'll have to pass by here, you monster, and you'll have to get out to move the tree. And if your two gorillas get out instead, then I'll shoot you through the car window!'

Don Camillo pedalled as fast as he could across the dry river-bed and got on the main road. 'Jesus,' he prayed, 'please give me enough breath and good eyesight.' He had pedalled nearly as far as the wayside shrine when a car passed him, but almost immediately had to stop, because the poplar beside the shrine had mysteriously toppled into the highway.

Don Camillo pedalled even faster, while the three passengers got out of the car and set about removing the obstacle from their path. He recognized Garrotte and raced to warn him, but he didn't reach him in time.

'Get out of there or I'll kill you too!' Flora shouted.

Don Camillo stopped in front of Garrotte and covered his body.

'I mean it, clear away from there!' Flora shouted furiously. 'And you two, stay where you are and up with your paws or I'll shoot!'

One of the two bodyguards had a bright idea and Flora gave him a warning volley at his feet which made him give a smart little hop.

'Get out of there,' Flora shouted for the third time. 'Garrotte, you don't scare me, Garrotte, the way you scared my father. And when you're dead, which is going to be very soon, there isn't going to be anyone about to say prayers for you.'

Flora had evidently gone mad, and to look at her face was chilling. But Venom, who'd come round from behind, saw only her back and so could feel no fear.

Flora was instantly disarmed and held up by the scruff of her neck, which took her breath away. 'Father, hold the gun while I take care of this maniac.'

Don Camillo came forward to recover his pistol, while Venom used his belt to strap the girl's arms to her sides.

'You creep, that bandit father of yours had me elected Queen of the Unity Festival just to give my father's murderer a good laugh!' Flora screamed, trying to free herself.

'If that hooligan's father is Peppone,' Garrotte said, after he had regained his composure, 'then he has a long way to go to make me laugh. But I'll have one for him pretty soon, the traitor!'

'In that case, why don't you try me on for size?' said Venom, dropping Flora and moving towards Garrotte menacingly.

Garrotte was truly capable of living up to his nickname, but the Russians, apart from teaching him to call the longhairs 'hooligans', had fattened him up like a pig, and Venom's first tap made the sweat ooze from Garrotte's every pore.

Venom was twenty-one years old and even though he was a longhair, he had a fearsome respect for his elders. Therefore he wasn't using his fists, only his open palms, and he had even put on his gloves for safety's sake.

One of the two gorillas had managed to sneak round behind the car and was stealthily making for Venom's back.

'Forget it, Falchetto,' Don Camillo suggested, waving the Browning. 'It's their business.'

When his gloves were nearly in shreds, Venom put a stop to the rubdown he was giving Garrotte. 'This is because you called me a hooligan,' he explained, 'but you'll have to see my father about the rest of it, because I don't get mixed up in politics.'

Garrotte and his bodyguards roared off. Soon afterwards, Bigio arrived with the truck, and Venom threw in Flora, Flora's motorcycle, and Don Camillo's bicycle. Don Camillo got in beside Bigio. Venom and his thundering motorbike escorted the truck as far as the rectory.

It was already dark, so Venom stayed for dinner. Flora didn't say anything until the very end. 'Would you be good enough to tell me why you butted in?' she inquired aggressively of Don Camillo 'Why didn't you let me kill him?'

'I had two reasons,' Don Camillo explained. 'First, we old priests are still somewhat hampered by the Commandments. Second, because if you had killed him, you would have gone to gaol for thirty years, and nobody would have given *you* an amnesty.'

Flora was not appeased. 'How can you say we young people have no call to rebel against your rotten society which worships murderers and picks on kids just because they wear their hair long? Do you really think we should go to war for your foul, filthy society?'

'Actually, you know the girl has a point,' Venom murmured.

Flora eyed him with disdain. 'Yes, I have a point, but you're going to go into the Army soon. Which is the way things should be: the Army takes care of poor sissies like you who are afraid of the putrid laws of this society of hypocrites. It takes more courage not to go into the Army than to go in like a sheep. And when they've shaved you bald, do you think you can still tour round sporting a leather jacket with "Venom" printed on the back?'

Venom, who was sweating under his wig, blushed and got up to leave.

'Good night, all,' he mumbled, and left.

'Is that the way to treat a man who stopped you from doing something stupid and irreparable?' Don Camillo chided her.

'I should be the sole judge of whether what I do is stupid or not, it's none of that wet's business!'

'I have already told you, he is not a wet.'

'All men are wets!' Flora declared fiercely.

Don Camillo was offended. 'Watch your tongue, young lady. Remember I'm a man too.'

'Since when do you have anything to do with it?' the girl snapped back. 'A priest is not a man. He's something less . . . or something more. It depends.'

Don Camillo was speechless. He had not expected a statement like that.

Devils are not necessarily
beings with horns and a tail

AFTER the highroad incident, Flora performed another
radical volte-face. She gave up all her idiosyncrasies and
took to dressing modestly, like a normal girl of old
bourgeois family. She seemed the essence of a decent,
pretty girl. She even went to all the religious functions,
causing Don Chichi – who, to tell the truth, had rather
diffident feelings towards her resulting from his treatment
by her longhaired friends – to admit to Don Camillo:
'Your niece seems like a different person.'

Don Camillo spread his arms and said: 'God only
knows.' Actually he was well aware of it himself.

Flora listened attentively to the little priest's ardent
sermons and one day, cautiously approaching him, she
confessed: 'Your sermons aren't filled with the usual
commonplaces, you talk about God without forgetting
men. I want to ask my friends to come hear you.'

Don Chichi started to laugh. 'I don't think your friends
like me very much, to judge by the way they set upon me
that famous afternoon.'

'The boys were wrong,' Flora explained. 'They took
you for another pious country-priest type like Don
Camillo. But you're not a parrot repeating the catechism
from the pulpit; you're not afraid of the truth. And by

79

the way, I can't understand why, while you bravely condemn war, all wars, you have never discussed the question of conscientious objectors.'

'It's a delicate question, Miss Flora.'

'I'm sure of that, Don Francesco. But there are priests who defend it at the risk of being brought before the Curia.'

'It's not a question of fear, but of respect,' the priest defended himself. 'Your uncle was a military chaplain and he has different ideas . . .'

'Wrong ideas!' Flora exclaimed. 'My uncle is a fossil! And as for respect, he certainly doesn't show much towards you! It strikes me as being quite dishonest, him sneaking off to celebrate clandestine Masses the old way in that chapel of his.'

'There's nothing clandestine about it!' Don Chichi answered. 'He tells me all about it. It's not really wrong if he gathers round his old altar those who won't come here any more because they're offended by my frankness.'

'I disagree, it's absolutely wrong! Don Francesco, what you are doing is to cast out the false Christians from the Church – and then he turns round and lets them in through the back door! You condemn them and he absolves them, thereby ruining the work you have done. As a matter of fact, what he is doing is stirring up dissidence in the Church, he's creating an opposition Church, an anti-Church! Don Francesco, you know it's true: to divide the Catholics is heresy!'

'You're blowing things up out of proportion!' Don Chichi exclaimed. 'However, a lot of what you say has some truth to it. Tomorrow I will speak on the subject of conscientious objection.'

'That's wonderful, Don Francesco!' the girl said, very moved.

The next Sunday, when he climbed up to the pulpit to give his sermon, Don Chichi was a bit taken aback: staring up at him were forty Scorpions, their leather jackets and long mops packed tightly together near one of the doors. They were poised to defend their motor-cycles, which they had left propped up against the façade of the church, with two sentinels to keep close watch over them. And Flora, wearing a modest dark dress and a shred of black lace on her copper-coloured hair, was there too, right in the middle of the front row of Scorpions, smiling at him. She was almost angelic.

Don Chichi threw himself directly into the fire. He condemned all wars, any wars, moving from Cain and Abel to Julius Caesar to the Crusades, winding up with Korea and Vietnam. Then he asserted that the only attitude a true Christian could take towards military service was conscientious objection. And he did not omit a nasty dig at men of the cloth who served as military chaplains.

The forty city-bred longhairs approved vehemently, nodding their city-bred bushes, and Flora's smile was so radiant that it would have dazzled a bishop.

After Mass, Flora went to congratulate the priest in the sacristy.

'I let them know,' she explained. 'And what I told them about you interested them so much that they came in spite of the huge risk they had to run. Don Francesco, you were marvellous! Those forty boys will go home much the better for listening to you!'

(Actually they went home much the worse for wear, since Venom and his rural gang were waiting for them outside the town, armed with great acacia stocks. It was like a film spectacular: Venom, heaven knows why, had a bone to pick with Ringo, the head of the Scorpions, and while two of the biggest toughs held Ringo tight, Venom gathered up his endless locks and shaved him bald as an apple.)

Flora was angelic, with all those tears brimming in her huge eyes: Don Chichi felt his heart fill up with tender-ness. Not for long, though: for Don Camillo, who had listened to the sermon hidden up in the organ loft, burst in, the veins in his neck thick as six-year-old grapevines.

'Don Chichi,' he snarled, 'better to be a military chaplain the way I was than chaplain of the thugs of the world! As for you, flower of darkness, get out!'

Flora began to sob and left, her head hanging. Don Chichi felt a wave of hatred for the reactionary, brutal, fat priest who made that meek and delicate creature suffer so. Seeing her shoulders shake with sobs, he suddenly imagined soft white wings sprout from them, and his indignation was so strong that he threw himself into his two-cylinder Fiat and fled to the city.

The next day, Don Camillo received a letter from the Curia that knocked the breath out of him. While he prepared for his transferment to Rughino, a remote mountain parish, and in order to forfend any heavier punishment, Don Camillo was called upon to: (1) Cease from causing secessionist subversion; (2) Cease from celebrating Mass in his private chapel; (3) Entirely cease from interference in the affairs of his parish, which upon his transferment would pass into the hands of Don Francesco.

Don Camillo caught a fever and had to take to his bed.

Clearly the devil is not ugly as he is in the paintings. In fact, the devil must be quite beautiful; otherwise how could he seduce and deceive people? In any case, the devil is always the devil, and in this particular case, there was no doubt about it, Flora was the devil. And when she heard poor Don Camillo was ill, she went to call on him.

'Most reverend Uncle,' she said immediately upon sitting down, 'have you any last requests?'

'Yes: I fervently hope you go to hell!' Don Camillo shouted. 'You may pack your bags and go home now.'

'Would you throw a poor orphan out on the street like that?' the dear little hoodlum whimpered.

'Not at all!' Don Camillo exclaimed, tossing her the letter which lay on his bedside table. 'It's you who have thrown me out!'

Flora read the letter and shrugged her shoulders. 'What's this got to do with me?'

'You got Don Chichi all fired up. I had no idea you were that evil-minded. And in the end you've won. How fortunate that your father is dead, so that he doesn't have to see what a reptile of a daughter he brought into the world. So now leave this house, or I will get out my shotgun!'

Flora went downstairs humming to herself, and as she left the rectory to go over to Anselma's, suddenly Venom blocked her path.

'Here's a little present from Ringo,' he said, dropping Ringo's mane at her feet.

'Murderer!' Flora howled, horrified. 'You've scalped him!'

'Not this time, but if he ever comes round here again, I will . . . Or rather, before he's able to get out of the hospital, his hair will come down to his knees.' Venom turned on his heel and stalked off; when he reached the gate, he turned and added: 'Anybody who listens to you will always get into trouble in the end. Don't let yourself be bitten by an asp like Cleopatra,' he growled. 'You'll poison the snake.'

With one furious kick, Flora sent Ringo's hair flying into a corner of the courtyard.

Just then Don Chichi arrived back. When Flora told him what had happened to Don Camillo, he was not at all pleased. 'I had no idea they would do that,' he said. 'They over-reacted!'

'Not at all,' Flora answered. 'They took exactly the right steps. I know Rughino, it's the perfect place for him. All the young people, men and women, have moved out to find work, and there are only the old fossils and the tiny babies living there now. So he won't be able to do any real harm there on the mountain-top. But this is a living town and it needs a young parish priest with modern ideas. Now Don Francesco, I hope you won't become sentimental and make me lose all the respect I have for you. However . . .' she broke off and drifted away after giving the priest a sad little smile.

83

She didn't turn up for two days. The first thing Don Chichi said to her was, ' "However" what?'

'Forget it, Don Francesco. If I'd told you, you would have been upset. It's not exactly a subject one discusses with a priest. Priests are born, not made!'

'That's not true, Miss Flora,' Don Chichi answered. 'I'm a priest not because I was "called" but through rational conviction. I realized how much good the Church can do for people who suffer. To nourish faith in those who have it, restore it to those who've lost it, bring it to those who lack it . . .'

'I understand,' Flora nodded. 'Faith is the most precious blessing. But in a world so different from that of two thousand years ago, in the materialistic world of today, you can only bring faith through deeds, not words. Too many promises have been made in the name of Christ. Humanity is tired of being promised paradise after death.'

'Miss Flora,' Don Chichi protested, 'faith helps one to live.'

'Not at all, Don Francesco. It helps one to die. If you haven't any shoes, even if you firmly believe that when you go to heaven you'll have a fine pair of golden sandals, your mortal feet get wet and you catch pneumonia. "O mortal soul who walkest on the crisp winter snows, in heaven wilt thou be given sandals of gold" – but in the meantime: "don't forget your galoshes." Don't you think that should be part of the proverb?'

'Well, it's exactly for that reason that the Church has tried to bring itself down to the level of everyday life,' Don Chichi exclaimed.

'Marvellous,' Flora said. 'But the people who die of starvation today, how are you going to cajole them into believing in heavenly banquets? Faith is the bread of the spirit, not the body.'

'Miss Flora,' the little priest tried to protest, 'forgive me, but this discussion has become rather too materialistic.'

84

'I admit that, Don Francesco. But the Pope should ask for money, rice, medicine, machinery to help starving India, not for faith and prayers. A few boring, trite material necessities.'

'Yes, but the Church can't . . .'

'Quite,' Flora cut in. 'The Church can't solve these practical problems. Don't you ever think about how much good you could do for people if you used your intelligence, your education, your enthusiasm, your persuasive, gentle way of speaking, your sincere, profound Christian faith in practical ways? You would never follow the footsteps of those vultures who use the name of Christ for political purposes – instead you'd use politics for Christian purposes!'

'But I . . .' Don Chichi stammered.

'Wouldn't you,' Flora went on, 'know how to treat workers well if you became an employer? Wouldn't you study the problems and propose good reforms for the poor if you were a deputy or a senator? Wouldn't you be able to keep the masses moving forward if you were a labour leader? Wouldn't you be able to formulate a wise foreign policy if you were Foreign Minister?'

'Well actually,' Don Chichi stuttered, 'I don't really think I . . .'

'But I do!' Flora shouted jubilantly. 'I know it! I'd give up all my life, all my inheritance, all my love if . . .'

She broke off and shook her head sadly. 'Forgive me. I'm saying some crazy things . . .' Then she ran off, sobbing.

A week later Don Camillo had calmed down, pulled himself together, risen from his bed, and was puttering about gloomily packing his trunks.

'What are you up to, oh esteemed reverend Uncle?' Flora asked, with her usual impertinence.

'I'm getting ready to turn things over to Don Chichi,' Don Camillo snapped.

'Well, forget it, because Don Chichi left last night.'

'Where has he gone?'

'I don't know. Perhaps he's going through that famous spiritual crisis that causes so many priests to leave and get married. Poor Don Chichi! He'll never come back here.'

'And what makes you say that?'

'I know it because I would shut myself up in a convent rather than marry an unfrocked priest.'

Don Camillo gaped at her, horrified. 'You!' he shouted. 'You serpent, you had the shamelessness to . . .'

'Well of course I did! I mean, you were hardly in a position to turn his head.'

Don Camillo's huge chest inflated fiercely. '*Vade retro, Satanus!*' he thundered. 'Go away! Leave me in peace!'

The girl looked at him, amused, and retorted laughing: 'Too bad, Uncle. Flowers come up, but they won't go away.'

Don Camillo raised his eyes to Heaven. 'Lord,' he said, 'will you ever be able to forgive this poor lost soul when she comes before you on Judgment Day?'

'It's hard to tell, Don Camillo,' the distant voice of Christ replied. 'It all depends on how her lawyer pleads her case.' But it was a distant voice, and only Don Camillo could hear it.

Old parish priests have bones of steel

THE east-west street through the town cut the large square at the centre into two rectangles, and one of these was furnished on three sides with a colonnade of thick stone pillars and was considered the vital property of the Church.

One morning some workers employed by the town arrived in the square and started to hack away at one of the columns with picks and drills. Two seconds later Don Camillo was on the scene.

'This is Church property,' he announced. 'Hands off.'

'The Mayor ordered us to . . .' the head of the crew began.

'Tell the Mayor that if he wants to tear down our columns, he can come round in person,' Don Camillo snapped.

In past years, Peppone wouldn't have hesitated to march into the square armed with picks, axes, drills, sledge-hammers, spades and anything else the job re-required. But even Communist mayors get old, so he took his time and didn't appear in the square until an hour later, driving a lethal-looking steam-shovel borrowed from the construction crew building a suspension bridge across the Po a few miles away.

He pulled the monster up a few yards away from one of the fat pillars and lowered the shovel. Then he got down, strung a steel cord around the pillar and connected it with the arms of the steamshovel. Then, just as Peppone was about to get back in the cabin of the monster, Don Camillo calmly clambered up and perched on top of the pillar.

Even though the Vatican Council has given all the power of the parish priests to the bishops and the laymen, it is still forbidden to uproot a fat column with a fat parish priest perched on top of it: so the square promptly filled up with townsfolk.

'Look here, you can't block public works voted in by the town council!' Peppone shouted at Don Camillo.

'Well, you can't tear down this column, which is on Church ground and which was put here by Father Antonio Bruschini in the Year of Our Lord 1785,' Don Camillo said, lighting up a Turkish cigarette.

But Peppone had an answer for that. 'Listen here,' he shouted, 'you forget that in 1796 this piece of land became part of the Cispadine Republic and therefore . . .'

'Therefore,' Don Camillo drowned him out, 'therefore if Napoleon didn't order these columns torn down, then it's hardly for you to pull them out, since you're quite a lot less important than Napoleon.'

Peppone had to give up because fairly soon Don Camillo was dragging out connections between Napoleon's wife and the Duke of Parma, Piacenza and Guastalla. However, two days later, the Bishop's secretary plunged into Don Camillo's office. The young priest, like all the progressive priests of the *Aggiornamento*, despised and detested all parish priests, and this sentiment was much aggravated by his knowledge of Don Chichi's poor showing.

'Reverend Father!' he ranted. 'Is it possible that you lie in wait for opportunities to show your obtuseness as regards political and social matters involving the Church? What is the meaning of this latest sideshow of yours?

Quite rightly Mayor Botazzi intends to encourage tourism and adapt the town to the needs of the motorized times – and to do this he wants to create an ample parking lot here in the square. How can you have the arrogance to oppose this project?'

'No arrogance at all: I'm simply preventing the destruction of Church property.'

'What Church property! You can't clutter half a town square with useless columns. Don't you understand what an advantage it will be to you? Aren't you aware that many people don't come to Mass because they can't find a place to park their cars?'

'Certainly I know that,' Don Camillo answered calmly. 'However, I don't believe the mission of a pastor of souls should be to organize parking lots and rock Masses to provide the public with a religion complete with all the modern conveniences. The Christian religion is not, and should not be, either comfortable or amusing.'

His point of view was a bit hackneyed and it caused the Bishop's priest to explode. 'My dear Father, you appear not to have grasped that the Church must attempt to bring itself up to date, and it should be helping progress, not blocking it!'

'But you, on the other hand, appear not to have grasped that your so-called progress has taken the place of God in the soul of too many people and the devil, when he tours around the city streets, no longer leaves behind the stench of sulphur but rather one of gasoline. The Lord's Prayer ought to be amended to read not "Deliver us from evil" but rather "Deliver us from prosperity".'

There was no point in arguing with such an old fossil, so the secretary wound up the discussion. 'Don Camillo, are you saying that you refuse to obey?'

'No, if His Excellency the Bishop orders us to transform the colonnade into a parking lot, we will do so, even though the Council has reasserted that the Church of Christ is the Church of the poor people and consequently should not have to worry about the cars of the faithful.'

Naturally, no orders ever arrived from the Bishop, much to the disgust of the Bishop's secretary.

Punctually every morning Smilzo deposited *Unity* on the rectory doorstep, and no less punctually Don Camillo skimmed through it with apathy, either because it was the official organ of the Communist Party or because it reminded him of the unfortunate circumstances by which Flora had won the free subscription to it. However, one day he was shocked to find on the third page a photograph of an altar surmounted by a crucifix, and beside it a blow-up of the crucifix itself. The photos were not particularly good reproductions, but there was no doubt about it, they showed Don Camillo's altar and crucifix. He quickly read the article, then jumped on his bicycle and sped over to his private chapel.

'Lord, Lord,' Don Camillo wailed, 'here's your picture in *Unity*.'

'So I see, Don Camillo,' the Christ answered. 'Let's hope I haven't made a mess for you like the ones your niece concocts. But if so, I had nothing to do with it.'

It was a remarkable tale, going back to 1944, when a troop of German soldiers was billeted in the town. Among them was an officer who, while he was supposed to be keeping his mind on the war, could not forget that he was a famous professor of art history. The Christ and certain of the altar ornaments had struck him and he had photographed them with extreme meticulousness. When he got home, he studied the photographs at length, discovering that the crucifix was a major work by a famous German artist of the fifteenth century, who specialized in painted carved wood. The German art historian after twenty-five years had returned to Italy to study and photograph the carvings in colour, but he hadn't been able to find either the altar or the Christ. So he had published his attribution anyway in a popular German picture magazine, using the photos he had taken in 1944. And *Unity* had reprinted article and pictures, with the simple comment: 'Where can the poor Christ have gone? Has he been forced to emigrate, like so many other poor Christs?'

Then other newspapers reprinted the article from the German magazine, and a minor scandal was brewing. Finally one day the Bishop's secretary plunged into Don Camillo's office a second time. He was indignant and confronted Don Camillo self-righteously. 'I see, Reverend Father, that you haven't given up trying to make trouble for us! Now where are the crucifix and the altar that are smeared all over the newspapers?'

'You ordered us to remove everything, and everything was removed,' Don Camillo answered calmly. 'In fact, you even sent us a political commissar to speed up the process.'

'It certainly might have crossed your mind that the object in question was a major work of art!' the secretary objected.

'We neither knew it nor suspected it, given our profound ignorance, since we are only a poor parish priest. However, by mere good fortune, we have taken the altar and crucifix into safekeeping.'

'Thank heaven!' the secretary cheered. 'Recover them immediately. Have them wrapped very carefully and when they are prepared for shipping, telephone us immediately. We will arrange for transportation to the Bishop's palace where they will have a dignified and proper home.'

Don Camillo nodded his head, the model of pious obedience.

'Mayor Botazzi . . .'

Peppone raised his head from the mountain of papers before him, and seeing Don Camillo standing there, clenched his fists.

'What do you want?' he growled aggressively.

91

'I'd like to talk to you about the parking lot. I've been giving it some thought and now I realize my position was unreasonable,' Don Camillo said. 'You can remove the columns.'

Peppone eyed him warily. ' "If a priest offers so much as a button, it can only mean he'll demand your suit in exchange",' he quoted. 'What's the deal?'

'Comrade Mayor,' the priest explained humbly, 'we have noted that for quite a few years now your Party has involved itself with enormous love and devotion in the major and minor problems of the Church. We would simply like to request that you and several of your comrades be present at the farewell ceremony for our precious crucifix, which after three hundred and fifty years of honourable service to our town is being moved to the city to a fine new home in the Bishop's palace.'

Peppone leapt out of his chair. 'You're out of your mind, Father! That crucifix is a work of art, and it belongs to this town! And it stays in this town!'

Don Camillo spread out his arms. 'I know, Mr Mayor. The problem is, however, that I have to answer to my Bishop, and not to your Party. Therefore I will have to hand the crucifix and altar over to the Bishop's secretary. I'm well aware that the Christ is a major part of the artistic and spiritual heritage of the town and that its place should always be the one it's occupied for the last three hundred and fifty years – on top of that altar in front of which you and many others took Holy Communion and were united in Holy Matrimony, in front of which your mother prayed while you were fighting in the War – your poor old parish priest understands all this, but all he can do is obey orders. And he will obey them unless of course he is threatened with violence. Because threatened with violence, what can a poor old parish priest do? Comrade Mayor, I beg of you, explain my plight to your superiors, and remember my position yourself, and realize that nobody could be more distressed at what I must do than I am.'

'Father,' Peppone shouted, 'if you think I'm going to sit still for this, you're out of your mind!'

Peppone was serious and the next morning the town walls were papered with mammoth posters denouncing the planned abduction and ending in two lines of big, bold lettering:

THE CHRIST IS OURS
NOBODY TOUCHES OUR CHRIST

Towards midday Don Camillo, who wasn't the slightest bit disturbed by the position Peppone had taken, calmly pedalled off to the private chapel in the old manor house lost in the countryside – and there a rude surprise awaited him. The toughest of Peppone's thugs were camping out in his garden full of weeds, passing the time pulling them up.

'You realize this is private property and I could have you prosecuted for trespassing?' Don Camillo said to Brusco and Bigio, who were in command of the detachment.

'Oh yes, Father.'

'May I go inside to wrap up the Christ and the pieces of the altar?' Don Camillo asked.

'You can go inside, but you're not wrapping up anything. You're a priest, not a freight dispatcher.'

'Well, I certainly don't want to break union rules,' said Don Camillo, bicycling off towards town.

The debate gained momentum. The newspapers devoted pages to the 'Embattled Christ'. Peppone held caucuses and summit conferences *ad nauseam* and littered the countryside with propaganda leaflets. It was the country in revolt against the city which always despises, deflowers and ultimately tries to destroy the country. Forgetting all their political rivalry, the entire town clustered round its Christ; even the atheists were talking about 'our Christ' and the artistic, historical and spiritual heritage that was being robbed.

Night and day the weed garden of the old manor house,

hidden away in its fields, filled up with people. And seeing that Don Camillo had accidentally left the door open, they could sleep inside well protected from the elements. A committee comprised of representatives from all the political parties and associations travelled to the city and made the Bishop give them an audience, during which Peppone voiced the respectful but adamant protest of the town's citizens. The Bishop heard all he had to say and then held out his hands smiling.

'But this is all a misunderstanding,' he said. 'There is nothing to prevent the altar returning to the place it has always been. The Mass can be celebrated in the new way in front of it, and the townspeople will have the additional inspiration of its exceptional artistic and spiritual merits. That is, provided that the parish priest has no valid reasons to oppose the restitution of the altar. The decision rests entirely with him.'

When the committee went to tell Don Camillo what the Bishop had decreed, Don Camillo answered humbly: 'We are fully prepared to carry out the wishes of our Bishop.'

It was a sweet autumn morning and the air and the fields were filled with the dust of gold.

During the night, a squad of volunteers had relocated the altar in the position it had been for several centuries and now the townspeople – all of them, young, old, men and women, no one left out – waited stretched out in two endless queues along the edges of the road leading to the lonely old manor house.

The brass band emerged from the gate and the sound of the cornets filled the golden fields. Following the band were about a thousand children, and behind the children marched Don Camillo, carrying the huge crucified Christ and striding along in measured, dignified steps. Behind him came the town flag-bearer and then Peppone, with a sash of the Italian tricolour, the town council bringing up the rear. As the procession moved along, the people lining the roadside fell in step and marched along behind.

The large wooden crucifix was heavy, and the leather strap under the foot of the cross cut into his shoulders unmercifully. And it was a long road. 'Lord,' Don Camillo whispered at a certain point, 'before you burst my heart, I'd like to get to the church and see you back on top of your altar.'

'We'll get there, Don Camillo, we'll get there,' the Christ answered, seeming to glow more beautifully than ever.

And in fact they did get there.

Today's young people
are a complicated bunch

A MAN who looked like a gravedigger arrived from the Ministry of Culture to inspect the famous crucifix that had been so much publicized in the newspapers, and once he had inspected it from top to bottom, he announced that he would send someone to collect it so that the necessary restorations could be made.

'The crucifix does not move one inch,' Don Camillo said through clenched teeth. 'There's nothing to restore.'

The gravedigger from the Ministry was accompanied by the Bishop's secretary, and when the young priest saw the steam coming out of the corners of Don Camillo's eyes, he leaped forward to say: 'Come now, Father, let's not talk nonsense. The Christ's right hand is broken off at the wrist and the crossbar is stuck together in the most haphazard manner with a rusty old piece of iron, probably by some poor idiot who had no idea what he was doing. Don't tell me you haven't noticed this.'

'Indeed!' Don Camillo snapped. 'It so happens that I am the poor idiot who fixed the crossbar.'

The Ministerial gravedigger was one of those zealous functionaries who are capable of blocking the construction of a bridge for twenty years if during excavation for the foundations so much as one potsherd dating from 1925 is turned up – on the other hand, should the Arch of Titus be uncovered, he would not open his mouth while it was being destroyed and a gas station put up in its place. He shook his head and laughed condescendingly. 'Now Father, let's not waste time. The man who comes to pick up the cross will give you a proper receipt for it.'

Don Camillo, with commendable frankness, explained to the gravedigger what he was going to do with that piece of paper, and reminded him that the door out of the church was the same that he had used to come in. However, the gravedigger was the many-laurelled holder of the well-endowed university chair on which he spent much time resting his ample hindquarters, and he raised himself to his full height and puffed out his chest like a quail. 'Father, I am the representative of the Ministry of Culture!'

'The Ministry of Cuture was not here, sir, on the morning of October 15, 1944,' Don Camillo answered. 'However, the people I represent were.'

'Father, spare us your little word-games!' the Bishop's secretary exclaimed, losing patience.

'No word-game intended – I have at least three hundred eye witnesses. If you like, I'll ring the bells and they'll all be here in a minute.'

Even though the young priest was from the mountain country, and even though the Ministerial gravedigger was from Rome, the two of them were well aware that in the Po river valley there are quite a lot of people who will flare up easily.

'Don't bother,' the gravedigger said. 'Just tell us instead.'

'It's a little story about the War,' Don Camillo explained. 'The Germans came to town and hid their Panzers and other vehicles beneath the trees of the streets, under the porticos and in the courtyards. There was someone here too who sent off secret wireless signals to the Allies about all German troop movements. So the liberators were quickly informed and their planes attacked the town one Sunday morning. It was an inferno. But nobody moved from the church, where Mass was being said. I didn't move either, but that says nothing for me because I'd been a military chaplain and I knew very well what a bomb can do. At the raising of the Host, a bomb exploded on top of the roof of the bell-ringer's house. A big piece of shrapnel came through the large rosette behind the altar – but Christ was watching over us, and He stopped the shrapnel with the right arm of the cross. Of course you laugh: the altar Christ is nothing but a piece of painted wood, but those men and women were not wooden at all, they were made of flesh and blood. Still their faith was greater than their fear and they didn't move a muscle. The piece of shrapnel broke off the end of the cross as well as the right hand of Christ. And the hand that was nailed to that piece of wood fell right in front of the altar rail and everybody saw it lying there, that poor disembodied hand. Well, the Lamb of God who takes away the sins of the world . . . In any case you understand my point of view. It's just a little war story, one that would have made the priests at the Council roar with laughter. But around these parts, people are fond of that kind of war story and so all of them – the old ones who remember, and the young ones who heard it from the old ones – will always have their eyes on that poor hand on the ground. And I'm just like those people. I'm an old priest and I hold that Christ shouldn't be forced to have plastic surgery to cover up the places where He has been wounded. That "rusty old piece of iron", as the honourable secretary justly called it, is actually the piece of shrapnel that cut off the wrist of our Lord. I had to drill holes in it to screw it to the back of the cross, which otherwise would have fallen down. After all, war has to serve some useful purpose.

Anyway, I understand completely, you can't listen to this sort of war story because you represent the State . . .'

'Not always,' the Ministerial gravedigger said. 'At times I'm called upon to represent myself. And as far as I'm concerned, things can stay the way they are. The crucifix is truly a magnificent work of art, but I don't believe there's any need to recommend that it have restorations done to it.'

'I'm completely in agreement with you,' Don Camillo answered, bowing.

Men have found a way of harnessing atomic energy, but no one had yet discovered how to harness the much mis-guided mind of Don Camillo's niece Flora. Now Flora had developed a new tactic. She kept herself locked up in the bell-ringer's house reading and scribbling, but from time to time she would come out, leap on her motorcycle and disappear.

Where did she go? Nobody had any idea. Don Camillo only had a bicycle and was in no position to go scampering off after his troublesome niece. So he decided to ask for help and the first time Peppone came by the rectory, he called him in.

'Comrade Mayor,' he said, 'I'd like to talk to your son Michele. Would you be good enough to tell him for me?'

'No,' Peppone answered. 'The only thing I'd be good enough to do to that kid is give him a smack on the head.'

'I'm appalled, Mayor. The town's been quiet for quite a while now. We haven't heard a peep from those pesti-ferous hooligans and we haven't seen a single manifesta-tion of your son's old ways – in fact, we've seen so little of him recently that it prompts us to ask if by chance he is ill?'

'In fact he is!' Peppone shouted. 'Ill in his head. Now that his turn's come, he refuses to go into the Army. He wants to be a draft dodger, spend the rest of his life running from the police!'

'Comrade, you should be proud of him!' Don Camillo exclaimed. 'Clearly Michele has listened to your anti-military speeches. As I recall, at your last town meeting, you said that if prisons were finishing schools for thieves, then barracks were the same for murderers.'

'I was talking about America and Vietnam!' Peppone protested. 'Michele heard of conscientious objectors first in *your* church, not in my town meetings!'

'I can't be held responsible for what Don Chichi may have said,' Don Camillo shouted. 'I am Don Camillo, and Don Chichi is Don Chichi!'

'Which added up makes two know-nothing priests who preach from the same pulpit in the name of the same God and one runs with the hare and the other hunts with the hounds!'

Peppone was easily excited and soon he was saying things about priests that would bring curls to the head of a bald man. Don Camillo answered in kind but suddenly, just as he was about to lose control, he regained his calm.

'Comrade,' he said in a placating tone, 'in this world, where everybody's always getting sick of everybody else, in this world dominated by selfishness and apathy, you and I keep fighting a war that's been over for a long, long time. Doesn't it make you feel as if we're just ghosts? Don't you have the feeling that in a short time, after having fought so hard, each for his own flag, we're going to be kicked out, you by your people and me by mine, and we're going to find ourselves reduced to our socks and forced to sleep under bridges and so on?'

'What's that got to do with it?' Peppone laughed. 'We'll still be fighting under the bridge.'

Don Camillo thought to himself that in a dirty, stingy world where it's impossible to find a true friend, it's some consolation having a true enemy, and he answered: 'Quite right, Comrade. But do send me Venom.'

Venom turned up, his face dark and his hair in his eyes.

'If you're hot, you can take off your wig,' Don Camillo told him.

'The wig's at home in the closet, man,' Venom answered. 'This hair's all mine. Even Samson's hair grew back.'

'I see. And like Samson, now you've regained your strength and are thinking about tearing the walls down again. Beginning with the Army.'

'I don't want to tear anything down,' the longhair growled. 'I just don't want to go into the Army, that's all. It's time we didn't have any more wars. We young ones want peace. If you want to make a war, you old people can fight it yourselves.'

'I don't want to make war,' Don Camillo explained. 'All I want to know is what the dickens Flora is up to. Every little while she disappears: I'm just afraid that she's back in with those toughs from the city. Do you know anything about it?'

Venom shook his bushy head. 'Actually I've wondered myself and once I went so far as to follow her. But she caught on and stopped to tell me to mind my own business. So I told her where she could go. And when you come down to it, I didn't have any right to go round spying on her.'

'While I, on the other hand, have not only the right but the duty,' Don Camillo declared. 'Rent a car and stick around. I'll pay you to do it.'

'No, just pay for the car. It's worth it just to annoy that mean little troublemaker. When the time comes, just give a whistle.'

Don Camillo didn't ever have to whistle. Two days later, when Flora jumped on her motorcycle and was off like a hurricane, Venom was in front of the rectory before she could turn the corner. Don Camillo climbed in and they were off in a cloud of dust. Venom drove like a man trying to make up a lap at Le Mans, and it wasn't long before Flora was in sight. She was touring along quite happily, oblivious of them, and they were able to follow her easily.

About eight miles from the city, Flora left the main road and roared off down a lane that meandered through the countryside. Venom turned too, and shortly Flora pulled up at a gate that had a long poplar avenue behind it. She went through and disappeared. Don Camillo and Venom found the gate closed and had to stop.

To the left of the gate was a little house. Venom pounded on the horn and the caretaker came out.

'Are you members?' the man demanded.

'Members of what?' Don Camillo demanded.

'If you don't know of what, there's no point in telling you,' the man growled. Evidently he had a phobia about both priests and longhairs. He withdrew into his gate-house.

The property was surrounded by a tall hurricane fence that came right up to the roadside.

'Let's go round till we find a way in, or at least work out what this place is,' Venom said, starting up the car again.

The property appeared to be a huge square plot of land; once they'd rounded the first corner, they found the same situation as before: ditch, high wire fence, and thick, thorny shrubs.

Venom stopped the car. 'Father,' he said, 'if you want me to, I'll take my shears, cut the mesh and go inside and take a look. I don't like the smell of this thing.'

'Not yet,' Don Camillo answered. 'First let's go round again.'

Just then they heard a motor roaring, and an aeroplane flying at not more than a hundred and fifty feet above them, came from somewhere in the middle of the fenced-off property and flew over their heads. They got out to look: the plane searched the area, then turned back and repeated its course, then went up to six thousand feet. Suddenly something separated from the plane, plummeted down for a few seconds, then a large white flower opened in the blue autumn sky.

'I can't understand these demented people who get a thrill out of sky-diving.' But since they were there, they might as well enjoy the spectacle. The little person hanging from the huge white umbrella manoeuvred it cleverly by means of the cords, and everything looked as if it was working miraculously well; but in a twinkling a fearsome wind blew up to fill the parachute and drag it off towards the river.

'That poor fellow is going to land God knows where,' Don Camillo said. 'Let's follow him.'

They got back in the car and went off in chase of the castaway. Venom muttered to himself, 'Typical priest. The minute there's a hint of being able to send somebody off to the Eternal Father, it's the end of sane thinking.'

The parachute was losing altitude slowly, and Venom, driving through lanes and byways and dirt roads like a lunatic, was barely managing to follow it.

'The high-tension station!' Don Camillo suddenly yelled, watching the parachute's stays swerve towards the electrical wires. However, if there's a God who takes care of fools, then the whole blessed Trinity must look after parachutists, because the flying bundle hurtled over the wires.

'That fellow's going to wind up in the Po!' Venom shouted soon afterwards.

Instead he wound up in a field at the foot of the embankment and the great white umbrella sagged down to the still green grass. Venom flew down from the embankment along a tiny dirt road, crossed a threshing-floor at full speed, scattering a flock of chickens, and finally found a tractor trail leading into the field. They found the skydiver wallowing in the moist grass; the little man had freed himself from the parachute harness and was now attempting to take off his helmet.

Suddenly sparkling in the sun, there were Flora's red

locks. Don Camillo covered the few remaining steps in kangaroo-like bounds.

'How can it be that you never do anything sane?' Don Camillo shouted.

Flora lit a cigarette and answered very sarcastically, 'This is not a sport for country priests or rural hoodlums.'

'And what makes it one for you?' Don Camillo snarled.

'If my father did it, why shouldn't I?'

'Your father did it because it was wartime and war makes totally insane demands of men!' said Don Camillo.

'My father did it because he wasn't chicken like some people. And anybody who's not chicken is all right, soldier or not.'

The men from the landing field had arrived, and they were obviously quite upset at the whole scene, so Flora reassured them: 'Don't worry, the only real mess-up is this visit from my reverend uncle the priest, with his altar boy in tow. You know how it goes: bad luck comes in threes.'

'You're quite wrong,' said Don Camillo. 'The only real mess-up was the fact that your parachute opened at all.'

Venom was frothing at the mouth and only found his tongue after he'd dropped Don Camillo off at the rectory. 'I'll show that snot-nosed brat just what kind of altar boy I am!' Venom snarled, and there was so much venom in his voice that even Don Camillo was a little worried.

Venom disappeared that day. It was only much later that Don Camillo heard Peppone speak of him – though actually, Don Camillo took the initiative to ask Peppone what had become of Venom, and Peppone answered: 'Only your God knows what's become of him! First, he refused to go into the Army and was all set to take a beating. Now, all of a sudden he's off a month ahead of time, going through fiendish machinations to get himself into paratroop training. You got that? Paratroop training? The idiots who throw themselves out of planes and fall to earth using flimsy pieces of cloth? Now I ask you, what in God's name goes on inside these kids' minds?'

'What can I tell you,' Don Camillo sighed. 'Today's young people are a complicated lot.'

'It's completely insane,' Peppone exclaimed. 'Naturally he doesn't care how much sleep we lose worrying about what might happen to him jumping out of planes hoping his parachute's going to open.'

'Actually the worst danger isn't that,' Don Camillo murmured.

St Michael had four wings

THE state of affairs in the bell-ringer's house hadn't
changed, but Don Camillo felt uneasy. Habit makes us
see things the way they no longer are, but the subconscious warns us of change. A certain relationship between volumes, solids and voids, light and shade is
thrown out of balance, and the rearrangement is immediately registered in the subconscious.

Don Camillo looked round the room for the fourth
time. Finally he discovered that the ancient miniature
of St John the Baptist was gone. Desolina said she knew
nothing about it and after a search in vain, Don Camillo
decided that the picture had been stolen and said: 'I'm
going to report the theft to the police.'

'If I were you, I wouldn't do it,' Flora said as she came
into the bell-ringer's house. Her leather coat was glisten-
ing from her long ride through the fog.

'And why not?'

'Because the picture's right here,' Flora answered,
taking the St John out of the bag she was carrying and

hanging it up on its nail. 'I took it into an appraiser in the city. He was prepared to hand over five sacks of gold for it – he offered half a million lire for it.'

'I'm not interested,' Don Camillo snapped. 'It was given to me twenty years ago by my old bishop, and it's dearer than my eyes to me. Why should I sell it?'

'To avoid gossip,' Flora said, calm and saucy. 'Look at it this way. The very reverend parish priest has his niece come round to be "re-educated", and what happens but the poor dear gets herself in trouble. Seeing as I can't go back to my saintly mother in this condition, unless I want her to have a stroke, I thought I'd go far, far away, find work, and serve up the brat myself. Naturally this requires lolly. That is, provided you don't want me going to town and working as a call-girl.'

'The only thing I truly, sincerely want you to do is to be struck down by God!' Don Camillo roared, horrified beyond his wildest imagination. 'I didn't believe even you could stoop so low.'

'Having a child has nothing to do with stooping low.'

'You impossible monster, didn't you think what you were doing to your mother?' Don Camillo shouted.

'Not at all: at the time I was thinking about what Venom was doing to me.'

'Venom! But you couldn't stand the sight of him!'

'The fact is I didn't have to look at him, as it was two in the morning.'

Her immodesty implored the vengeance of God, and Don Camillo clenched his fists. 'There's no way out of it. This time I'm breaking all your bones.'

'Would you dare strike a woman in my condition?' Flora huffed indignantly. 'Ah, but you've never been a mother and don't know what it feels like . . .'

Don Camillo was a man of quick decisions: he fled at a run from the girl's temerity, and once in the garden, he opened the curtains from outside, and through the thick bars of the window he said: 'Keep clear of this window because if you come within arm's length, I'll strangle you.

107

Now, answer me: was it really that rapist who got you into trouble?'

Flora sat down in front of the fireplace and lighting a cigarette, she puffed on it calmly. 'I'm in no trouble, dear uncle. The one who's in trouble is you. And there are no rapists involved: it's obvious that if I hadn't wanted to, Venom wouldn't . . .'

'Venom!' Don Camillo thundered, rattling at the bars. 'That delinquent is going to have to answer for his deeds. There will have to be a wedding immediately!'

The girl sneered. 'Oh really, dear reverend Uncle, suddenly we're back in the middle ages, when, to save the honour of the family, girls of fourteen were forced to get married? Then go on endlessly bringing brats into the world like rabbits, after that set themselves up in the middle of the town square or in the doorways of the streets with tin cups just because, according to them, society owes them room and board? Is this your Catholic morality? How can a marriage between two stupid kids be considered a sacrament? Is this respect for the institution of the family? It's a hundred times more immoral for two kids with no sense of responsibility to get married than to let two hundred unwed mothers run round loose. It's just because I respect my family and marriage that I will not marry a screwed-up idiot like Venom. Redemption by marriage indeed! To heal a wound, you cut out a heart. My God, how can one take you people seriously? To drive a pitiful two-horsepower Fiat, you've got to pass a ten-page exam and get a licence, but to get married and present the world with a herd of kids, something a thousand times more important, far more serious and dangerous for society, all you have to do is say "Yes" in front of some good-for-nothing fat priest!'

Plastered against the window grille, Don Camillo was going through torture, sweating furiously, seething with rage.

'I'm going to have you locked up in a girls' home,' he spat.

'As of yesterday, I'm legally an adult, holy holy Uncle. And now nobody's going to tell me what to do.'

Don Camillo tried the iron bars with his teeth, and then shouted: 'Take the damn picture and sell it, and then go straight to hell!'

Flora put out her cigarette on the floor, stood up, took the picture, put it back in the bag, and made for the door. 'O.K. Uncle, see you,' she said. 'If it's a boy, you can bet I'll call it Camillo.'

Peppone's wife had made up her mind: she wanted a mink. Not an opera diva's mink, you understand, but just a little stole which didn't cost more than a million lire. Peppone had set himself against it.

'Imagine it. They're already accusing me of going bourgeois, and now you want me to buy you a mink!'

'Now look, we don't live in China, and there are no Red Guards here.'

'Now *you* look, we do live in this town, and there are a thousand cranks here, each one of whom would give his eye teeth to say I'd eaten the People's money and got rich off their blood, sweat and tears.'

'That's nonsense. The shop is yours and you paid for it with your money, not to mention mine.'

'Maria! Can't you understand that if I go out into the square and make speeches about the sufferings of the people and then turn round and buy you a mink stole, that disqualifies me?'

'Well, stop making speeches about the sufferings of the people. They couldn't be suffering less and they're all driving round in cars etcetera. And whether or not anybody's suffering has nothing to do with whether or not I have a mink coat instead of a wool coat.'

Just then somebody knocked and Peppone had a chance to catch his breath. His wife went to the door and came back, followed by Flora.

'Mayor,' said Flora, 'I'd like some information.'

'Go over to the town hall and ask for the community secretary,' Peppone answered.

'I can't,' Flora explained. 'The father of the child isn't the community secretary's son, he's the son of the Mayor.'

Peppone looked at her, open-mouthed. 'Are you out of your mind?'

'Not at all. According to the obstetrician, I am expecting a child.'

'Well, go and wait for it as far away from here as possible!' Peppone's wife shouted fiercely.

'I'd be delighted,' Flora came back calmly. 'Seeing as my uncle has thrown me out and seeing as the father of the child, Venom, that is, is in the Army, I'll go over to the town hall and wait for it on the steps.'

'I cannot for a moment imagine that my son Michele had relations of that sort with you!' Peppone stated curtly.

'It's not quite so difficult for me to imagine,' Flora snapped. 'And in a few months it will be a little less difficult for you to imagine, too.'

Peppone's wife was rabid. 'You can talk over with my son these things,' she screamed. 'Now get out of here!'

'Just a minute, Maria,' Peppone intervened. 'This one has no morals and she wouldn't think anything of involving us in a scandal.'

'Exactly what my uncle said, and he put up half a million lire to get me out from under foot.'

'You blackmailer!' Peppone's wife howled. 'That's what you're up to, taking advantage of my husband's position to soak us! You think you can force my son to marry you!'

'Marry?' Flora sneered. 'Is it likely a pretty girl with her head screwed on right would stoop to marry an idiot hoodlum like your son?'

Peppone rushed to prevent his wife from throttling Flora and said: 'Well, if it's not marriage you're after, may I ask just what it is you want?'

'I'd like to leave here, find a two-room flat, have the

child, and bring him up by myself. I haven't the slightest intention of bringing a family of foundlings sired by your son into this world. I have my dignity, self-respect and principles to think about.'

'Listen to her!' Peppone's wife wailed. 'She talks about dignity and principles after what she's done!'

Flora had sat down and lit a cigarette. 'Quite so, Signora,' she answered smiling. 'I did with your son exactly what you did with your husband. That is, unless your eldest son was a medical phenomenon born in four months. The difference between us is that I won't humiliate myself by whining and howling and threatening to throw myself under a train if somebody doesn't marry me!'

'I never once threatened to throw myself under a train!' the woman protested.

'That's true,' Peppone admitted. 'She threatened to throw herself into the Po. Now, girl, will you tell us what you think you can squeeze out of us?'

'I don't want to squeeze anything out of you. All I want is an honest job.'

'Job? I don't have any jobs to give you!'

'Mayor, my reverend uncle's money has allowed me to buy a nice pickup van and to rent two fine rooms at the Rocchetta. I'd like to go round from door to door selling your goods, and on every piece sold, you would give me a commission.'

'But why don't you apply to the manufacturers for a dealer's licence?'

'I've tried that, but everywhere they want me to put up a certain kind of personal contribution which I do not want any part of. And please understand, it will appear as if I am competing against you, not working for you.'

The girl's perfidy had no bounds. She had overheard Peppone's argument with his wife from the porch, and scurrilously taken advantage of it.

'Don't be astonished, Mayor. I know people. They get more pleasure from other people's misfortunes than they do from their own good luck. The peasant gloats when his neighbour's harvest is poor. In church, it's the same: many people behave piously not for the pleasure of going to heaven but for the pleasure of knowing how many others will go to hell. The same goes for politics. Your proletariats, who have nothing, fight not to better their own situation but to worsen the situations of people who have a great deal. Now why, Mayor, given that we can't count on the goodness and intelligence of our neighbours, don't we also take advantage of their wickedness and stupidity? And why, instead of sending your wife around the countryside looking like a washerwoman, don't you buy her a fine mink coat and a fat, sparkling diamond ring? Mobs of people would begin to hate you, and instead of buying your goods, they'd buy from me. And we'd both have a thriving business.'

'If I were you, I'd try it,' Peppone's wife advised. 'This hellcat has as many tricks up her sleeve as the Devil himself.' An optimistic and erroneous statement, for Flora had at least two more than the Devil.

Flora, lovelier, more perfidious and flamboyant than ever, launched her ship and inundated the region with washing-machines, dishwashers, refrigerators, television sets, transistor radios, and similar merchandise.

The people, who weren't aware of the enormous volume of business the clandestine subsidiary was doing, were delighted to see less and less people frequenting Peppone's emporium. And when they saw his wife Maria sporting a mink stole and a flashy diamond ring, they sniggered with anticipation of the moment when she would have to pawn ring and stole to stop the leak from the store.

After four months, Flora had set up an immense clientele and everything was moving along swimmingly, when suddenly out of the blue, Venom came home on a weekend pass.

He returned theatrically, in the way things are always

done in the operatic nation: Peppone was speaking from the podium in the town square, denouncing the Vietnamese war and American military barbarism. He was wrapped up in what he was saying, and his diction was clear and pure, as though it had been engraved by Bodoni. But suddenly he saw something that left him with his jaw hanging. There in the first row was Venom, in the uniform of the Paratroopers. He seemed at least seven feet tall, and Peppone maintained that all he lacked was two wings on his shoulders and a sword in his hand to be the Archangel St Michael.

Vietnam suddenly didn't matter, the U.S.A. even less, and he cut his speech short. 'And so let's end today by giving three cheers for Liberty: Hurray for Liberty! Hurray for Liberty! and hurray for Liberty!'

Peppone's wife lacked her husband's control and decided that Venom actually did have two wings on his shoulder and a sword in his hand and there was no question in her mind at all that he was St Michael the Archangel. She even detected a little gold halo round her son's brow. And naturally she burst into tears and said the only thing she absolutely should not have said: 'Oh Michele, what are you going to do with that poor dear Flora? If only you knew how brave she's been and how hard she's worked . . .'

Venom said he didn't know a thing about it and his mother explained that the girl was expecting a child and that he shouldn't go round distributing his flesh and blood all over the place.

Venom jumped on his motorcycle and roared over to the Rocchetta. He found the poor dear girl on the Avenue and there was a light fog which imparted a fairy-tale atmosphere to the scene.

Flora was driving her pickup full of electrical appliances when Venom cut her off. She went white and gripped the steering wheel as tightly as she could. She tried to catch her breath, the poor dear – it's no everyday occurrence, running across Saint Michael in the street like that, complete with two wings, a halo and a flaming sword in his hand.

'H-home on leave?' Flora stammered, trying to make small talk.

'Yes. They tell me you're expecting a child by me.'

'Funny, I heard the same thing,' Flora admitted. 'But actually I'm not expecting anybody's child.'

'That's good,' Saint Michael said, flashing his sword threateningly. 'Still I don't understand what made you tell your uncle and my parents anything of the sort, particularly since there's never been anything at all between us.'

Flora decided that Saint Michael's wings weren't that overpowering and his sword wasn't flaming and returned to her former self. 'Even I have a right to a place under the sun, don't I?' she answered. 'I had to find something to do! Otherwise, how could I have squeezed the money out of my uncle and got your father to give me a job? Or do you think you're the only one with a right to live?'

'No,' Venom growled. 'But just this: why me?'

'Why me?' Flora mimicked aggressively. Suddenly she'd developed a flaming sword too and looked like Joan of Arc. 'Who do you think you are? I thought you were supposed to be fighting this absurd world created by moralizing criminals the same way I am. Even if we belong to different gangs, aren't we essentially alike? Answer me, Venom the Great Rebel – don't you just love this disgusting world that the old fools have built and would like to foist on us? Does it really seem to you that these dirty old hypocrites deserve respect? Don't tell me the Army cut off your rebellious spirit as well as your hair?'

'No!'

'Well then, why not use these old fools and liars to build a world that's worth living in? The shameful old hypocrites fear one thing, and that's scandal, right? Great! So I terrorized them by threatening them with scandal. I just used you as a pretext, and the reason I used you was because I thought you were one of us. Aren't you? Are you angry? Do you want to run home and tell them it's not true, that you haven't got anything to do with it, that you're a good little boy while I'm a nasty brat? That's fine with me. Go ahead!'

'No,' Venom answered. 'I haven't changed and I still believe we have to stick together. The way I see it . . .'

'Yes?'

'Since you told them you're expecting my child, the way I see it you ought to go through with it. It would, shall we say, validate the protest.'

'I'm opposed to extremism,' Flora protested. 'And besides, you're not my type.'

'And who would your type be?' Venom bridled. 'That scab Ringo? I'll beat his face in.'

'Don't you dare. He helped me sell a refrigerator to his aunt, a dishwasher to his sister, and a washing-machine to his brother-in-law. And besides, I never said anything about Ringo being my type.'

Venom shook his head. 'I don't understand why you don't think I'm your type.'

'It really bothers you?'

'After all, I run the town, I'm the best racer in the area, everybody thinks I'm great.'

'Like me?'

'There's nothing great about you, you're just crazy. Also, I can do judo and I'm learning karate.'

'A definite step in the right direction,' Flora admitted.

'Speaking of the child,' Venom went on, 'when they see nothing's happening, how are you going to explain that?'

'I already have my route and my clients. But for the moment, it would be nice if you went along with it.'

'Naturally. "Venom's a good kid and doesn't side with the enemy".'

'Are you staying long?'

'I'm going away again tomorrow. If you want, I'll give you my address. You might need it.'

'That's unlikely, but give it to me anyway. Here's my business card.'

'Great. You might even be able to sell my barracks a fridge.'

Flora's business card in his pocket, St Michael plucked a feather out of his wing, wrote out his address on it, and handed it to Flora. Then he left without saying a word. That's how kids are these days: hard. Heartless, even.

Watching him walk off, Flora counted four wings, not two. 'I *know* I'm not seeing things,' she muttered as she rounded the corner, nearly stripping the gears.

That's the way the sheep baas

DON CAMILLO was roasting chestnuts in the bell-ringer's fireplace, when suddenly a voice made him jump out of his skin: 'Good morning, holy holy Uncle!'

'I thought we agreed you weren't to set foot in here ever again,' Don Camillo said without turning round.

'In fact we did,' Flora admitted. 'But when I heard you needed me, I swallowed my nausea and came.'

'*I* need *you*?' Don Camillo shouted hysterically.

'Not me personally, but a two-hundred litre fridge with a freezer compartment.'

Don Camillo pulled the frying pan out of the fire, jumped to his feet, and squared himself off in front of the girl. 'You and your fridges can go straight to hell!' he shouted threateningly.

'Don't I wish we could,' she retorted. 'What a land-office business I'd do down there.'

She pulled a catalogue out of her bag and thumbed through to a certain page, flattening the book out on the table. 'Now this is the model I had in mind for you. Twelve monthly payments: you won't even be aware of paying them.'

'Why on earth do I need a fridge?' Don Camillo roared.

'Well, first of all, because it's a huge bargain, with the

117

discount I'm giving you. Secondly, buying it from me, you're doing Peppone out of business. Thirdly, you can give the fridge to me as a wedding present when I get married.'

Don Camillo's jaw dropped. 'Ah, so now you're getting married!'

'Well obviously someday I'll get married. Do I seem to you the type who couldn't get herself a husband, when there are so many morons running around?'

Disappointment fired up Don Camillo's anger again. 'So there's no chance at all of avoiding a scandal!'

'You mean it wouldn't be a scandal if a girl brought a child into the world two or three months after she'd been married? Is this the kind of morality you were taught in the seminary?'

'Do we have to start this all over again?' Don Camillo howled, pounding his fist on the table.

The girl was infinitely impudent and finally Don Camillo lost his temper. 'Shameless hussy, first you rob me of my St John and now you want to blackmail me for eight thousand lire a month?'

'Any other uncle, or at least one who wasn't a priest, would do at least that to help out a poor orphan niece who was pregnant,' the tiresome brat quavered.

Flora was very beautiful even though she was cynical and disrespectful; but now a shadow of sadness veiled her eyes. And the fact was, she had gained weight and puffed out.

'Just sign on the dotted line,' she explained. 'I'll leave it for you to think about.'

'All right, I'll think about it,' Don Camillo growled.

'Great,' said Flora. 'Now let's go into the shop.'

'What shop?'

'Yours. I want to confess.'

'You mean you are going to make *me* listen to your confession?' Don Camillo squeaked, horrified. '*Me?*'

'Of course,' Flora said, calmly peeling a chestnut. 'If Mary Magdalene was heard by Christ, why shouldn't a miserable little parish priest like you listen to me? Don't tell me you think you're better than Christ!'

'No!' Don Camillo stormed. 'But I'm your mother's brother and I just don't know what to make of a niece like you!'

'The fact we're related has nothing to do with it. I'm a sinner and I'm here to confess to the parish priest.'

'Find another parish priest to empty that black well of yours into!'

'No, most holy Uncle. You know all the facts and it's simpler to tell you.'

'I refuse! How could I have the proper spirit of serenity listening to you? I couldn't get rid of my perfectly justifiable resentment, I couldn't judge you with the proper impartiality!'

'The hell with your judgement, Father. You're not the Almighty. You just listen, take counsel with the Almighty, and then He will decide. I know what's bothering you: that picture of St John. Priests all despise money. Other people's money that is, but when it comes to their own, watch out!'

'The picture doesn't matter at all. I'd have given everything I have to get you out from underfoot. Your immorality appalls me!'

'Honest work is not immoral,' Flora retorted. 'And the work I do is honest because I do it in broad daylight!'

'When I say immorality, I refer not to what you do in broad daylight but to what you perpetrated in the dark of night and what will very soon cause a poor fatherless wretch to be brought into this world. Furthermore, I despise your conscious malice. I know what your nasty game is: to get even with the man who got you in trouble, you're setting about as best you can to ruining his parents by robbing them of their clients.'

The girl laughed. 'I'm not robbing anybody of anything. I know how to sell better than they do and I sell more than they do. They wait for the mackerel to jump into their nets, I go and seek them out where they live.

It's the same thing with you. You parish priests hide in your rectories all tucked away comfortably in armchairs like income tax collectors, waiting for the sheep to come in. The trouble is, people have to go to the income tax collector to be shorn, otherwise their furniture is confiscated and they find themselves in the clink. But no law forces them to come here. Now look, dear Uncle, if you want clients, you've got to go out and get them the way I do. New priests like Don Chichi understand this and they go to the hotels, places of entertainment, and into the factories to get after the workers. They learn how to drink, to play poker, to swear, dance the "Monkey", and hate the capitalists. Sometimes they even get married to avoid becoming bureaucrats the way you old parish priests have.'

'If you've come here to make sacrilegious speeches, you can leave right now!' Don Camillo snarled.

'I came here to make a confession. And if you refuse to hear my confession, I'm going straight to the Bishop's secretary to lodge a protest.'

'All right,' Don Camillo fumed, as he stalked off towards the church.

Flora knelt at the confessional. 'Father, bless me for I have sinned,' the wretch said. 'First I would like to confess the sin that weighs most heavily on my mind, because I committed it with malice.'

'Speak, my child; I will hear you.'

'I took advantage of the naïveté of a poor parish priest and led him to believe that I was expecting a child, for the express purpose of making him give me money that I needed to start up my little business. Furthermore, this morning I tied a sheet around my waist and padded it to keep him fooled so that I could sell him a fridge. Then I confessed the whole hoax to him here in church to prevent him from punishing me.'

'Dear child,' Don Camillo replied, with great effort, 'last year a hoodlum who had held me up in an alley pulled the same trick on me. I respected the secrecy of the confessional but it didn't prevent me from giving him a kick in the seat of the pants afterward.'

'To err is human, to forgive divine,' Flora warned him. 'But I'm not sure God will forgive you this time.'

'Dear child, I hope, with the help of God, to succeed in cleansing myself of animosity towards you. Do you mean, then, to say that you and that young man never had any sinful relations?'

'Neither with him nor with anyone else,' Flora affirmed. 'I'm ashamed to say it, but it's true.'

'Do you mean to say that, appearances notwithstanding, you have some moral principles?'

'No! Your morality nauseates me. All I'm saying is that the right bloke hasn't come along.'

'Dear child, you're on the road to damnation. Sin doesn't come only with acts, you know: words, thoughts, and omissions can also be sinful. It's sinful to create a scandal as you have done. It's not any more sinful for a girl physically to commit a sin; it's also forbidden to act like a sinner. In your case, you've committed a mortal sin not so much by fooling your poor uncle, but by accusing an innocent young man of a grave lack of propriety. What is he going to say, when he finds out you've accused him falsely?'

'He already knows it,' Flora declared. 'He and I have talked about it.'

'And what did he say to you?'

'Well what *could* he say, poor dear. He said it was all right with him.'

'Dear child, does it seem right to you, the damage you might do to that poor boy's reputation?'

'But I'm not doing him any harm!' Flora protested.

'You obviously want to marry him; that much is clear. Do you really think his offence merits such heavy punishment?'

'I don't want to marry him to punish him, I want to because I like him!'

'And if you don't want to punish him, why are

you working so hard to ruin his father's business?'

'I work for Peppone,' Flora confessed. 'I'm competing with his shop, but all the merchandise I sell comes from him.'

Don Camillo mentally called upon the Christ. 'Lord in Heaven, please help me. It's the first time the devil himself has come to confess. What can I do?'

'Don Camillo,' the distant voice of the Christ answered. 'You must find out whether the girl has repented her acts or not. Everything depends on this.'

'Dear child,' Don Camillo asked Flora, 'do you repent what you've done or not?'

'I wouldn't dream of it,' the brat said. 'What's the point of repenting something that's worked out so perfectly?'

'Do you hear that, Sir? Not a whit of penitence!'

'Well it was exactly what I expected her to say,' the Christ answered.

'Go, you are forgiven,' Don Camillo whimpered. 'Your penance will be three Our Fathers, Hail Marys, and Glorias, to be said in front of the Virgin's altar in the riverside chapel. Now go quickly, child! Have pity on a poor old parish priest who's racked with the temptation to come out and cover your face with slaps!'

Don Camillo's voice revealed his inner turmoil, and Flora raced out of the church as fast as she could. A few moments later, Don Camillo heard her pickup drive off, so he emerged from the confessional to confer with the Christ over the high altar and unburden himself of the sadness in his soul. 'Dear Lord, if the young people make a joke out of the most serious things in life, what on earth is going to become of your Church?'

'Don Camillo,' the Christ said in a reassuring tone, 'don't let yourself be carried away by what appears on the television and in the newspapers. The fact is, God does not need men. It is men who have need of God. Light exists even in a world of the blind. As somebody once said, "Though they have eyes, yet they cannot see."

The light won't go out just because there's nobody to see it.'

'Well, Sir, tell me why that girl acts like that. Why does she extort, rob, steal and cheat to get something she could have just by asking for it?'

'Because, like most young people today, she's dominated by the fear of being judged an honest woman. It's the newest kind of hypocrisy: once upon a time, dishonest people went to great lengths to be judged honest. Now honest people go to equal lengths to be considered dishonest.'

Don Camillo spread his arms. 'Lord, what is this insanity? Does it perhaps mean that the great circle is about to close and the world is rushing towards self-destruction?'

'Don Camillo, why are you so pessimistic? Was my sacrifice in vain, then? Do you mean that my mission among mankind has failed because men's malice is stronger than the goodness of God?'

'No, Sir. All I meant to say was that these days people only believe in what they can see and touch. But there are essentials that cannot be seen or touched: love, goodness, piety, honesty, purity, and hope. Most of all, faith. Things which one can't live without. This is the self-destruction I was talking about. It seems to me men are wiping out their entire spiritual heritage, the only true fortune they have accrued in thousands of years. One day not very long from now, men will find themselves back in the brutalism of the caveman – the caves will be skyscrapers filled with the latest equipment and miraculous machines, but men's souls will be primitive and brutish. Lord, the people now muster great armies who terrify and ravage and disintegrate men and things. But perhaps only those armies can restore men's true richness to them: they will destroy everything and men, liberated from their earthly well-being, will turn to God again. And once they find him, they can reconstruct the spiritual dominion which today they are bent on destroying. Dear

Lord, if this is really what's happening, what can we do about it?'

The Christ smiled. 'The same thing the farmer does when the river floods his fields: try to save the seed. When the river goes down, the land comes out again and the sun dries it. If the farmer has saved his seed, he can sow it in his field, which is even more fertile now that the lime-filled water of the river has soaked into it. And the seed will take root, and the fat golden spikes will give men bread, life and hope. The point is to save the seed, which is faith. Don Camillo, you have to help those who still have faith and keep it intact. The spiritual desert every day grows broader, every day new souls dry out because they're abandoned by faith. Every day men of many words and no faith are destroying the spiritual heritage and faith of other people. Men of every culture and religion.'

'Sir,' Don Camillo asked, 'do you mean to say that the devil is so clever these days that he can dress as a priest?'

'Don Camillo!' the Christ reproved him, smiling, 'please, I just went through the agonies of the Vatican Council, do you want me to go through even more torture?'

'Forgive me, Sir,' Don Camillo apologized. 'My head is full of wind. What can I do?'

'You could sign the agreement for the fridge.'

'Don't tell me you've gone in for electrical appliances too.'

'Not I, Don Camillo, but that poor girl has.'

Don Camillo went back to the rectory all confused. He still couldn't believe he had heard the Christ right when He said 'poor girl'. Anyway he signed the contract but it was quite a chore because, perhaps from the smoke from the fireplace, perhaps from the diabolical sulphur fumes Flora had left behind, his eyes were full of tears.

Remembering a May day long ago

WHEN DON CHICHI had disappeared one day, Don Camillo had notified the Curia, but they had replied that they knew about it and he shouldn't worry.

Don Camillo had not worried; hardly, since what worried him was the little priest's presence, not his absence. So he never gave the matter another thought, until four months later when he ran into a mountain priest whom he'd known in the seminary, who told him that Don Chichi, shortly after his disappearance, had been assigned to the tiny parish of Rughino, which was to have been Don Camillo's punishment.

'He's a regular whirlwind, that one,' the mountain priest went on. 'You know Rughino's practically a ghost town because the men and women who have any brains or strength find work outside, leaving the ancients to care for the children and houses. It's only three kilometres from Lagarello, my parish, but until a few weeks ago, to get to Lagarello from Rughino was a nine-kilometre journey, just because there's no straight road with a bridge. It's the same story with half of those towns. Well, one day all the ancients helped by the older children started to work like madmen and now they finally have a decent road. All on account of your Don Chichi, who took the initiative, studied the situation, organized the workers, and then took up the pick and shovel himself.'

'That's magnificent!' Don Camillo said. 'It ought to be a great satisfaction to Don Chichi.'

'Yes and no,' the priest answered, laughing. 'The fact is, now that there's a road, the people of Rughino, rather than sit through Don Chichi's moralizing sermons, trudge six kilometres, back and forth, to come to my Mass. But I think if they play him right, Don Chichi will build an entire network of good roads through the mountains.'

Doubtless this was a good idea, but the Curia wasn't aware of it and so, a little while afterward, Don Camillo was called before the Bishop in person.

'Our Don Francesco,' the Bishop explained, 'is completely cured. He has suffered a spiritual crisis and we sent him to recuperate in Rughino where he has brilliantly succeeded in accomplishing great things, among them to convince his flock to build a bridge and road they had needed for years. We inaugurated it along with the civil authorities and the regional prefect paid enthusiastic compliments to Don Francesco in his speech.'

'I'm delighted!' Don Camillo said. 'Truly a triumph of persuasion.'

'A triumph in many ways,' the Bishop amended. 'The fact is, thanks to Rughino's being linked to Lagarello now, we have been able to eliminate another useless parish. Therefore, Don Francesco having completed his mission, he is again free and can return to be of service to you, Don Camillo.'

'Well actually,' Don Camillo stammered, 'we don't have any road problems . . .'

'Don Camillo,' the Bishop cut in, 'your long experience united with his youthful enthusiasm will give new life to your parish. And while we're on the subject, we would like to suggest to you that you find more suitable accommodation for your young niece who, if you'll forgive us, does not seem to us to be the proper sort of girl to be running around inside a rectory.'

'The young woman,' Don Camillo, who had begun to sweat, explained with control, 'has always been a guest of the bell-ringer's family. Besides, for several months now she's been living in another section of town.'

'So we've been told,' the Bishop nodded. 'All we wished to make clear is our advice to you to keep her as far as possible from your rectory. We say this for obvious reasons. Do you understand us?'

'No, Excellency,' Don Camillo said.

'Don Camillo,' the young Bishop exploded, 'apart from everything else, the girl's political bias makes her presence at your church somewhat inopportune.'

'I understand, Excellency,' Don Camillo said with great effort, 'but the girl herself is not responsible for the fact that her father was assassinated by the Communists.'

'No, but our aim is not to keep hate alive, but to help expunge it. The girl's presence is an obstacle to coexistence. She is the living proof of a past that is being forgotten. In any case, she's not exactly the kind of girl you want associating with your Daughters of Mary.'

'Perhaps not,' Don Camillo admitted, 'but she's just a modern girl, a bit high-spirited, but honest.'

'Honest!' the Bishop exclaimed, shaking his head. 'Fire's honest too, but you don't make a practice of putting it near petrol!'

Don Chichi appeared at the rectory a few days later and surprised Don Camillo in the throes of a work of great moment: he was toiling away over a sign for the church door, and had so far printed the words MASS FOR THE REPOSE OF THE SOULS . . . The pen was a bit difficult to handle, given Don Camillo's huge hands, so Don Chichi offered to help out.

'May I be of assistance, Father?'

'Thanks,' Don Camillo answered going on with his work, 'His Excellency warned me that you are convalescing from a serious illness, and I wouldn't want you to tire yourself.'

'Don't worry!' the priest exclaimed, laughing. He took the pen from Don Camillo's hand and set to drawing the letters. 'My illness is a long way off!'

In fact his illness was right at hand and came into the rectory just then. 'Good morning, holy reverend Uncle!'

Hearing Flora's voice, Don Chichi went white and jumped to his feet.

'Well, Don Francesco!' Flora chimed angelically. 'You've finally come home! You've no idea how much we've needed you here!'

'That remains to be seen!' Don Camillo exclaimed, thoroughly irritated. 'As for you, there's no need at all for you to be lurking about. So get going!'

'I've brought your fridge,' Flora said, her voice full of tears.

'I don't want any fridges!' Don Camillo shouted. 'I'll pay you as we agreed, but take that contraption home where you can use it to stuff that codfish you're marrying!'

'Uncle, please,' Flora protested, blushing furiously. 'I'm not thinking at all of getting married. In fact, I've decided to become a nun.'

'You're crazy!' Don Camillo roared.

'Must one be crazy,' the girl demanded, 'to feel the need of praying for the salvation of men who have lost their fear of God?'

Flora's unbelievable temerity forced Don Camillo to lose his temper. 'I don't want to hear any more! Get out before you bring more trouble into my house. The Bishop doesn't want you around the rectory!'

'Why not?'

'Because he doesn't like you!'

'His Excellency has never met me,' Flora said with an angelic smile, 'but the Good Lord knows me and I shall try to make Him like me. Uncle, why is it that you want to put out the holy flame of faith and renunciation in me?'

Don Chichi, who meanwhile had gone on with his work drawing the sign, now said: 'Father: MASS FOR THE REPOSE OF THE SOULS – I've written that out. What else do you want to follow?'

'OF THE DEAD WHO FOUGHT IN HUNGARY,' Don Camillo grumbled. 'It's the thirteenth anniversary of the Soviet repression in Hungary.'

Don Chichi put down the pen and shook his head. 'Don Camillo,' he said in a tone that reflected all the indignation mustered in him by Don Camillo's barbaric treatment of his small, fragile niece, 'you've lost touch with the world. Haven't you noticed that the press, magazines and newspapers included, in recalling the tragic days of Budapest, has placed the accent – and rightly so – not on the repression but on the rebirth of Hungary?'

'I'll brew beer out of your reborn Hungary!' Don Camillo shouted. 'Those poor men crushed under the treads of Soviet tanks haven't been reborn, and neither have the eighteen-year-old boys who were sent to prison and "legally" executed for protesting against the repression!'

'Don Camillo,' Don Chichi said in firm tones, 'all that is part of the past. God thinks about the dead. We should be thinking about the living, because peaceful coexistence can only be brought about among the living. Why rekindle old hatreds? Why poison the souls of young people who don't even know what happened in Budapest thirteen years ago? God is love, not hate. The Church teaches that we shall love our enemies.'

Don Camillo's ears turned red. 'It's been nearly two thousand years since Jesus was crucified,' he said, 'and still today the Church represents him as crucified on the Cross. Not to make people hate the enemies of God, but to remind them of Christ's love and sacrifice!'

Flora chimed in, 'Reverend Uncle, if you'll notice, the new liturgy tends more and more to omit representations of Christ in agony and religious art is leaning away from the crude realism of the crucifixion. Don Francesco's idea is quite apt. Jesus suffered as a man and died as a man for love of mankind. Of all men, it was primarily those who had actually crucified Him whom He forgave on the Cross. Keeping up the old tradition of wax-museum realism in depicting Christ's martyrdom on the Cross only kept alive hatred for those who had crucified Him. Reverend Uncle, doesn't it mean anything to you that the Pope and the Council solemnly absolved the Jewish people of deicide, after nineteen centuries of anti-Semitism and oppression? And while we're on the subject, why remember the dead in Hungary any more than the six million slaughtered by the Germans?'

'Because the German murderers are almost all dead or punished,' Don Camillo raved. 'They no longer are a regime that threatens the liberty of the entire world! Because Cardinal Mindszenty is still under house arrest, and he represents the oppression of the Church, the Church of Silence!'

Don Chichi smiled. 'The Church of Silence doesn't exist, because God is everywhere and speaks to anybody who wants to listen.'

'All right then,' Don Camillo bellowed, dripping with sweat, 'what's the purpose of the Church? Why did the Son of God descend to earth to suffer and die like a man? In any case, you write what I tell you to. I'll think about the rest of it!'

Don Chichi, delighted to see the fat old priest billowing fumes and sweat, snapped back tauntingly: 'Don Camillo, I see there's another blank card. I imagine that you'd like to fill it with an announcement for a High Mass on May 8th.'

'Of course! You wouldn't want me to ignore VE-Day, would you?'

'Victory in Europe,' Don Chichi spat with disgust. 'A black day in human history. There are no victories in war! We should forget that and all other commemorations like it. In war, everybody loses and everybody's in the wrong.'

'I want to remember the souls of the people in that war,' Don Camillo shot back.

'The same old story, the same old dead men,' Don Chichi said sarcastically. 'This makes the Church into a grave-robber who spends his time in the cemetery of history unearthing hardened bones and putting them in a display case. Father, what is this morbid religion of yours, with its lugubrious slogans? "We are born to suffer"; "Remember that death comes to all" . . . No! Remember that you must live! This is the meaning of Jesus's revelations. It's the meaning of the Resurrection!'

Flora gazed at Don Chichi with ecstatic eyes. 'Don Francesco,' Flora said, 'you've struck right to the heart of things. This is why kids today won't have any part of the Church – because the Church spends its time talking about dead people, because it only teaches you how to die, not how to live. Because it denies men all rights and loads them down with duties. Because it won't admit the concept of earthly happiness and maintains that Paradise exists only in Heaven. At the same time, it maintains that anyone who lives according to God's law and the social proprieties can find happiness on earth too. And then it creates for priests a bunch of mangy crows who think the birds that chirp on a bright spring morning fall deeper into sin with every note, when actually they're singing praises to the Lord!'

'Flora,' Don Camillo hissed, 'will you stop being stupid!'

'It's true, Uncle. Look at that sweet Soeur Sourire, who sings about God, accompanying herself on the guitar and millions of people's eyes filling with tears listening to her – didn't they force her to leave her order? Wasn't it the mangy crows that cast her out? – Don Francesco, would you have done such a thing? You're a bright young priest, educated and modern, would you have stopped that nightingale from singing the praises of the Lord?'

'Never!' Don Chichi exclaimed, very moved.

'Don Chichi,' Flora went on in a caressing voice, 'leave the old priest to his cadavers – it's the only thing left of a long, useless life. Make up his posters for him. Some old fossils will undoubtedly turn up at the eighth of May Mass; but there won't be a soul at the one for the Hungarians. Then maybe the old fogey will understand it's not the time for dead people, but for the living. If it's any comfort to you, I'm entirely and whole-heartedly in agreement with you.'

'That's enough for me!' Don Chichi said, going back to work.

Flora turned to Don Camillo, who hadn't stopped gaping at his incorrigible niece.

'Hey Unc, where do you want the fridge put?'

'I don't really care,' Don Camillo whispered.

'I'll have it put in your bedroom. That way, instead of going to bed every night, you can climb inside the fridge, and you'll keep ever so much better. The orthodox Church needs a lot of well-preserved corpses.'

Don Chichi sniggered.

Don Camillo went off to supervise the unloading of the refrigerator. Then when Flora was climbing back into the pickup, he stopped her.

'Fiend,' he hissed in a low voice, 'what plans have you got up your sleeve for poor Don Chichi?'

'To sell him a fridge,' Flora replied simply.

'Keep far away from here! Don't you get me into trouble with the Bishop!'

'Don't get nervous, Unc. I'll sell the Bishop a fridge too.'

'Don't say things like that, even as a joke.'

'Why not? I sold the Bishop's secretary a fridge to give to his sister. Why shouldn't I sell one to the Bishop too?'

Flora zipped off in her pickup and Don Camillo turned his eyes towards heaven.

'Dear Lord,' he said, 'what do you make of all this?'

'How should I know,' the distant voice of the Christ replied. 'I don't know anything about fridges.'

*

The night before the Mass for the Hungarian Dead, Don Camillo received a letter in which the secretary by order of His Excellency stated his disapproval of the politically inopportune gesture. He also received a crate which contained a colour photograph, beautifully framed, of Cardinal Mindszenty, tagged with a small card:

Compliments of
Flora Electrical Appliances

Don Camillo threw the letter into the fireplace and went to hang the portrait over the main doorway under the Mass announcement.

Don Chichi watched him do all this, then after Don Camillo had climbed down the little stepladder, he shook his head and said, looking at the portrait of the Magyar Cardinal, 'Why do you have this urge to make a martyr out of yourself? Even him, couldn't he have found a way to live with the authorities in his country?'

'Take pity on him,' Don Camillo. 'He got out of line because of that other rowdy who got nailed up on a cross. The usual business that goes with extremists.'

It was a strange Mass, because apart from the few old cronies who could find Masses to attend even if they were celebrated inside the Rock of Gibraltar, there wasn't a single cleric present, a sign of the Catholic hierarchy's disapproval of the initiative antagonistic to the Church's movement of dialogue and non-militance. In recompense, Don Camillo had the entire Socialist contingent, who were there to show that in spite of their Marxism they thought quite differently from the Communists.

Peppone and his henchmen were there too: they had come to show that in spite of their Communism, they were made of quite different mettle than the Soviet and Chinese extremists.

Don Camillo's sermon was short and sweet: 'Brothers, much has been said about dialogue between people who stand on opposite shores. The souls that we are here today to remember stand on the shore of Death, and are speaking to those of us who remain on the shore of Life. Let us listen to what they are saying to us, and our hearts will find the proper answer. Amen.'

The great river was brimming with limey water, and all the people coming out of the Mass went to the banks to see whether the water level was rising or going down, and they remembered Don Camillo's simple words.

Some of them straightaway saw the blood-red glow on the waters near the other shore.

A little boy who saw angels

A SCRAWNY little boy was struggling along in the mud on the highway, and on his bony shoulders he carried a bag that appeared to contain something very heavy. The quiet, and the black, bare trees that stood out like ghosts from the chilly fog, then melted back into the grey, made the atmosphere seem part of another century and the scene reminded one of the story of Tobias or at least *Les Miserables.*

Don Chichi, pulling his Fiat up beside the boy, rolled down the window and said, 'Where are you going?'

'To Piletti's farm,' the boy answered, resting his sack on the roadside wall.

'It's a long way in this cold.'

'I don't care,' the boy answered with a timid smile. 'I like walking alone in the fog because then I can talk to the angels.'

Don Chichi helped the boy in with his sack.

'It's rather heavy,' the boy said. 'It's potatoes, the little ones that the peasants set aside for the pigs. I earned them doing odd jobs. They gave me a pumpkin too. Pumpkin, you know, cooked in with the coals is very sweet, and my little brothers and sisters love it.'

'There are that many of you?'

'Five sisters and four brothers. But Citti, my older sister, works in the city. She's sixteen already.'

'What does your father do?'

'We live alone with our mother. Our father is dead.'

'But how do you manage to live?'

'We don't know, Father. Only the Good Lord knows, but it's enough for us that He knows. Turn right here, we live down there in that yellow house.'

It was no house, it was a miserable lean-to. Inside the only room, which was divided in half by a shaky wall made out of grapepickers' baskets, seven children were playing around a woman whose pitiful clothing hardly served to cover up her well-developed thirty-year-old body. There were no beds, only straw mats, and no furniture, only fruit crates. The only luxury was a ramshackle old iron stove, obviously filched from some junkyard.

Don Chichi was saddened and indignant, and said that it wasn't possible for human beings to live in such squalor.

'Father,' the woman replied, 'we really don't mind. It would be enough for us if the landlord would fix the roof, which leaks all the time, and put a window into that wall, because it's always dark as night in here.'

Piletti's house wasn't far off and Don Chichi went there with his jaw set. He found the old farmer in the stables and attacked him immediately: 'Don't you think it's your duty to do something for those poor people?'

Piletti spread his arms out. 'And what can I do, Father? I went to the Mayor, I went to the Police, and they all said I'd have to deal with it myself. The only thing left to do is rip the roof off the house, but I'll have to wait till spring to do that.'

'Rip the roof off?' Don Chichi howled, horrified. 'Your duty is to repair that roof, put some windows in, build some sanitary facilities – in other words, make that shack fit for human beings to live in!'

Piletti gaped at him. 'That slut with her tribe of mewling bastards crept in one night from God knows where. I found them camping in my woodshed one morning, and when I tried to get them out of there, the woman started to scream that this was no way to treat victims of the flood, and since the babies were yelling as if I'd tried to tear out their insides, I had to let it pass for the time being.'

'And you don't feel the slightest responsibility towards those poor souls who had everything taken from them by the fury of the waters? Didn't you see the devastation wrought in the flood areas on your television?'

'Of course I did,' the old man roared, 'but the floods happened in 1966 and these people arrived here last June!'

'Misery is the same every year, sir!' Don Chichi affirmed. 'Here is a poor widow with nine children and society has very clear duties towards those poor people!'

'Well, I'm not society!' Piletti shouted. 'I'm only the tiniest fraction of society, and it's not fair for all of society's burdens to weigh on me alone. Those people appropriated my woodshed, they steal from my orchard, they eat my chickens, they burn my wood, they milk my cows, they make off with my linen – and you say I should fix their roof and put a window in their wall and make the woodshed comfortable to live in? Listen, we can barely scrape up a living ourselves, and me, my wife, and my daughter work like slaves on this farm!'

'That poor widow is young and hearty,' Don Chichi observed. 'Why don't you give her work?'

Piletti let out a wail. 'Father, this past summer, when it came to the tomato harvest, I had her and her oldest children working, I paid them union wages, and those ingrates denounced me as an exploiter of widows and orphans. They had an inspector from the Department of Labour come round, and between the fine and what those brats ate, it cost me a cow. As if that weren't enough, when I reported the forcible occupation of my woodshed to the Police, it was to protect myself against further lawsuits from the Department of Labour, who were about to prosecute me for not giving a salaried, resident employee a contract, working papers, health insurance, profit sharing and a whole slew of other rubbish!'

'But it's the State's duty to defend the workers' rights!' Don Chichi protested.

'And I suppose employers are a bunch of good-for-nothing bums who scratch their bellies for a living!' the old man roared.

'Christ has said: "Woe unto those who deny the worker his just due".'

'I know,' the old man shrilled, 'but that doesn't say his just due is a Rolls Royce! All these workers who come in to pick ten grapes for you suddenly aren't satisfied with a Fiat or a Volkswagen and want you to provide them with Rolls Royces to drive to work in!'

Don Chichi was indignant. 'Shame on you!' he exclaimed. 'Making fun of the miserable conditions of the working class!'

But he left, because at that moment Piletti had introduced his pitchfork into the argument and seemed prepared to use it to clinch the debate.

Don Chichi felt himself entrusted with a sacred mission, and after describing the plight of the widow and her orphans, he said: 'Don Camillo, we disagree about many things, but here you must stand beside me. Insofar as we can, we must help those poor people.'

'Don Francesco,' the older priest answered, 'I have one or two things to say on the subject, but I will restrain myself. Now that woman had nine children. We can take the youngest ones into the parish orphanage and give them clean clothes and something to eat.'

'That's something at least, Don Camillo, but I think about that poor boy who was walking barefoot talking to the angels. He seemed quite sensitive and intelligent. Let's take him in with us. He can be the altar boy, he can bring around announcements to the people in the parish, he can keep the church and rectory tidy. We'll give him decent clothes and food and what little money we can spare. Reverend, he said the most beautiful thing to me when I asked him how they managed to live: "We don't know how, only the Good Lord knows, but it's enough for us that He knows." That boy hasn't let poverty and hunger and hard luck embitter his heart, which is what usually happens. His misery seems to inspire him, in fact, and bring faith in God, and it lets him talk to the angels. If we were to help him, we would nourish a calling in him that would probably make a fine priest one day. A true priest of the Church of the Poor, because he was born and has lived in poverty. Don Camillo, remember Matthew, where Christ identifies himself with the poor: "I have been hungry and you have given me to eat . . . I was naked, and you have clothed me . . . To the extent you have done so for the smallest of my brethren, have you done the same unto me." Don Camillo, remember Matthew and then remember Mark, Luke and John: "Who so-ever shall take a child like this one into his arms, shall take me in as well . . ." '

Don Camillo remembered Matthew, Mark, Luke and John, but forgot the rest of it.

Marcellino proved to be what Don Chichi had predicted. He was a perfect altar boy, and sang joyfully in the choir. He haunted the rectory all day long, always ready to jump on his bicycle to do an errand. He was gentle in manner and in looks, and on Sunday when he carried the collection plate through the pews, his smile squeezed coins out of the stingiest churchgoers. He spent long hours in the church talking to the angels or reading books Don Chichi lent him.

One Sunday morning, after Mass had ended, Marcellino came up to Don Camillo in the sacristy, and holding out the collection plate full of money, said in a sweet, humble voice: 'Father, it's time to talk about cuts.'

'Cuts? What cuts?'

'My cut,' Marcellino answered, smiling. 'I collect the money and I have a right to a share of it. I deserve fifty per cent of it, but I'll settle for forty-five.'

Don Camillo gaped at him, perplexed. 'Marcellino,' he said finally, 'did the angels tell you this?'

'No, Father,' the boy admitted, 'I talk about other things with the angels.'

'That puts a different light on things,' Don Camillo said, showing him the door with a kick on the seat of the pants. 'Try not to let your face be seen around here ever again.'

Marcellino disappeared without a word, but his mother turned up that afternoon. She was in full fighting trim, and came forward in traditional battle phalanx, the youngest child in her arms, the four and five-year-old daughters clinging to her flanks, and the other four children bringing up the rear guard. They invaded the rectory, and with dramatic gestures she pointed to her unhappy tribe, saying: 'Father, you are ruining us by sending Marcellino away, just now when my poor Citti has lost her job in the city.'

Don Camillo spelled out the predicament more clearly. 'She didn't lose her job, she lost her fourteenth job, and now she's going to have to change her line of work.'

At that time, slogans were all the rage, and a very popular one was: 'The employer is always wrong.' For that reason there were people like the aforementioned Citti, who got herself hired and after a while behaved so badly that her employer was forced to fire her. Then she would hotfoot it over to the Unemployment offices and denounce the employer for countless infractions of the labour laws. Instantaneously, efficient functionaries would descend on the employer, confiscate his ledgers, put all his worldly goods under lock and key, and uncover unforgivable breaches of the labour laws, which

140

they punished with enormous fines and 'adequate compensation' for the deprived worker. It was a very ingenious system for avoiding work while still counting on an income and, more important, for making the despicable employer suffer. Citti had pulled this stunt fourteen times and had always got away with it, so that now, understandably, nobody would hire her.

'It's not her fault, poor dear, if all she's ever found is dishonest bosses,' the woman protested. 'You can't throw Marcellino out: I'm a poor widow with nine children to feed!'

'Nobody forced you to bring them into the world!' Don Camillo pointed out.

'Father!' the woman exclaimed indignantly. 'I'm not one of those sluts who uses the Pill!'

'I'm sure,' Don Camillo said calmly. 'You're just a slut who's brought nine children into the world without ever having a single husband, and then you presume to demand that society should support you! Get out of here!'

The woman left howling, vociferously supported by the squeals and whimpers of her seven children.

Don Chichi, who'd been watching the scene without comment, now protested vigorously. 'Don Camillo, a poor woman who's protecting her young ones shouldn't be treated like that.'

'She's not a poor woman and she's not defending her young ones but asking to be defended against them. Too many people bring herds of children into the world only to hide behind their hunger and suffering. What a filthy racket that is!'

'But it's not the children's fault!'

'I'm not blaming the children for anything,' Don Camillo said. 'I'm only saying there's no point in encouraging, or worse, praising – which is what happens all the time now – their appalling parents. What we must do is prevent them from turning their children into so many enemies of society.'

Two days later, a furious functionary from the

Department of Labour descended on the rectory.

'You,' he said to Don Camillo, 'had in your employ a thirteen-year-old boy and you made him work even on holidays.'

'Serving Mass is not work,' Don Camillo said. 'It's voluntary participation in a religious rite.'

'Any activity producing something is work,' the functionary declared.

'Mass produces nothing concrete or material because it is a spiritual process,' Don Camillo said.

The functionary laughed. 'The theatre doesn't produce anything tangible either. However, it is an amusement and so there's such a thing as Actors' Equity whose members are protected by the labour laws. Unionwise, Mass can be considered a theatrical performance. The boy performed an essential function in it and should have been paid accordingly for his labour. And in fact he is entitled to overtime for working on holidays. He should have been given severance pay, and furthermore he should have had the proper working papers for employees of public institutions as well as a Social Security number, and you should have taken out health insurance for him.'

The functionary was the typical bureaucratic bully who was accustomed to see employers shake in their boots. Therefore he was a bit taken aback when Don Camillo showed him the door, saying, 'I understand your problem and I will say a prayer for you.'

'You're quite wrong, Father, if you think you can get away with this!' the functionary shouted.

' "To err is human",' quoted Don Camillo, as he swung the door shut on the functionary's nose.

Naturally, the bulletin board outside the Workers' Home carried a fierce attack against Don Camillo, who preached neighbourly love and proceeded instead to drive a poor boy out into the cold without giving him his just due.

Peppone didn't let well enough alone, and hired

Marcellino as delivery boy at his electrical appliance store. He complied with all the union rules, giving the boy all the papers and insurance necessary; and he made sure that everybody in town heard about it, too.

Marcellino behaved like an angel, so much so that one day Don Chichi pointed it out to Don Camillo. 'You see, Father, I was right. Marcellino is a fine boy and you just didn't understand him.'

'That's possible,' Don Camillo admitted. 'I wonder if he can see angels among the fridges and washing machines?'

The truth was, Marcellino no longer saw angels, but he was still very perceptive and he saw, hidden inside a washing machine, a certain tag marked *Confidential* and took it home to study more carefully.

Then he let Peppone know that if he wasn't given 150,000 lire, he would be forced to bring the tag over to the district tax collector who made a hobby of uncovering this sort of 'confidential' registration tag.

Peppone couldn't allow himself to be accused of not respecting his duties towards the working classes, and he decided to take the money over to Marcellino's mother himself, to recover the registry tag.

He found the poor lady confined to her bed, in the throes of bringing her tenth child into the world.

Yet another tale about the great river

ONE Friday night, at about eleven o'clock, Flora received a phone call from Tota, one of the Scorpions' girl friends. 'Flora, what have you done to Ringo?'

'He kept bothering me, so I told him to jump in the river,' Flora explained laughing.

'He's blown his top and is determined to get even. He knows where all Venom's boys live and he's coming over to rout them out one by one and tear them to pieces. The attack's set for tomorrow; as soon as they cut out, I'll call you.'

Flora knew how nasty Ringo could become when he forgot to be a human being, so she scampered over to warn Venom's three lieutenants.

The three rural toughs shrugged their shoulders and said they didn't know what they could do about it.

'Well, for one thing, you can go round and warn everybody. Tomorrow morning everybody should wait for me at the Macchione at seven sharp.' Then before she went home, Flora knocked on Peppone's door.

Peppone was getting ready for bed and said in no uncertain terms that he didn't want to talk about electrical appliances at that hour.

'Neither do I,' Flora said. 'Just give me Venom's black leather jacket and help me load his motorcycle into my pickup. Tomorrow a bunch of Scorpions are coming down here to start a punch-up.'

Peppone's ears turned red. 'Not those lunatics again? I'll let the armory know and we'll arrest the lot of them and put an end to this!'

'Don't get mixed up in it,' Flora said. 'This is our business. Just hand over the junk and go to bed and dream of Stalin. Maybe he'll give you some good numbers to play on the lottery.'

At seven the next morning, the gang of rural longhairs was gathered in the deserted Macchione valley. Without Venom they felt like powerless schoolboys. It was freezing cold and they had lit a huge brush fire to warm themselves up; but fear is the kind of chill you can't drive out of your bones with brush fires.

They talked the situation over and after an hour they reached a decision: to climb on their cycles and head for the hills.

Just then they heard the powerful, familiar sound of a Harley and everybody jumped up.

Flora floated inside Venom's jacket and was even more lost on top of the enormous Harley: still, the sight gave everybody the shivers.

'They're on their way,' Flora announced. 'Thirty of them, so that makes us even. They're coming by different roads so no one will notice them, but the plan is to join forces halfway along the highway, and what we'll do is wait for them behind the embankment wall and when they turn up, we'll scalp them all! Okay, let's go!'

Flora was inspiring. The first thing she did was perform a tricky and dangerous spin-out, then as she pulled on to the highway, the boys could see the white skull and lettering, and every one of them cheered and shoved off with an energetic kick, ready to set the world on fire.

The tip-off was spot on, and the first few Scorpions to reach the highway were taken care of in a flash. But when the bulk of them arrived, the fighting got rough. Flora was giving orders from the top of the embankment wall. She had spotted wire barrels filled with rocks, intended to reinforce the river wall, and since her men were losing their nerve, she called up four of the rural longhairs and gave them each a pair of pliers. 'Cut that meshing,' she ordered. 'It's time to bring on the artillery.'

The four country hoodlums obeyed Flora as unhesitatingly as the French army had obeyed Napoleon, and this was obviously going to be the turning point of the battle. 'Listen to me, men,' Flora shouted as soon as she saw their hands full of rocks as big as melons, 'you see those balloons covered with long, greasy hair that the Scorpions have tied to their shoulders!'

'Flora,' Ringo shouted, 'I warn you, if I get my hands on you I'll brain you!'

A big stone bounced off his ear: an inch more to the right and that would have been the end of the head of the Scorpions.

The young man went white. 'Oh, so you want to fight dirty, eh!' he shouted. 'All right, we can play serious games too! Men, let's see those blades shine!'

The Scorpions pulled out their flick knives; the rural longhairs drew back and suddenly they all were swinging bike chains. In another minute, somebody would have been killed. The two gangs were lined up face to face, waiting motionless for orders from Flora or Ringo to attack and begin the massacre.

But the order never came, because a thunderous voice exploded into the silence: 'Drop all that filth you have in your hands!'

Peppone and his high command had appeared on the ridge of the embankment with double-barrelled shotguns.

'Brilliant,' Ringo sneered, 'to stop the punch-up, you're going to kill us.'

'Who wants to kill you?' Peppone asked. 'Our cartridges are full of salt. Lead works better, but if you'll recall salt has a certain salutary effect. So if you don't throw down that junk, we'll salt you up for good!'

Just then Don Camillo appeared on the ridge.

'Father, get out of it!' Peppone roared. 'This is none of your business!'

'Yes it is. If one of these idiots dies, I'll be here to give him Extreme Unction.'

'Throw down your weapons!' Peppone shouted. But he was a little worried, because he knew he wouldn't be able to fire into them point-blank.

Flora sensed this and shouted: 'Well, don't just talk about it, shoot!' she said, grabbing the shotgun out of Peppone's hands and aiming it at Ringo.

The longhair went white and dropped his switchblade. 'Get that gun away from her!' he shouted. 'She's not kidding, she'll shoot! I know her, if she weren't like that I wouldn't have picked her to be my girl!'

Flora laughed nastily. 'You stupid worm! I've never been your girl and I never will be. I'll be whoever's girl I choose.'

Ringo started to laugh. 'Snotty brat! When a Scorpion picks a girl to be his, the girl's his and nobody else's. That twit who wears a jacket with a skull painted on the back of it was stupid enough to look at my girl and is going to pay for it with his whole gang of goons!'

'I'd say the truth is, she looked at him,' Don Camillo corrected Ringo. 'Anyhow, that's no reason for you to start trouble with your whole gang.'

'It's plenty of reason,' Ringo shouted. 'An insult to one Scorpion is an insult to all Scorpions. That's our code. And why isn't your big hero here anyway?'

'He has better things to do. Besides, wiping out a dope like you is something I can handle myself!' Flora said as she pulled the trigger.

Don Camillo knew it was going to end this way, so he was ready for it and just in time his huge hand slapped the barrel down and the cartridge full of salt ploughed into the ground separating the two gangs, raising chunks of turf.

Both gangs had thrown down their weapons and Smilzo went round collecting knives and bike chains.

'So,' Don Camillo said, 'you're the youth group, the protesters. Do you come round here making trouble to protest too?'

'Why no,' Ringo answered. 'It's as good a way as any to dump your putrid laws and put our own into effect.'

'And what laws might those be?' Peppone inquired.

'The law of survival of the fittest. It's the law of nature. The weak ought to be done away with.'

'I see,' Don Camillo snapped. 'Yesterday I read in the newspaper about an eighteen-year-old boy who murdered his parents because they bored him.'

'He's not one of us,' Ringo declared. 'Because for us, all parents are already dead. They're walking, talking corpses. Even your laws forbid murdering dead people. Desecrating graves, like that.'

'Tell me, who are these living dead?' Peppone asked, seething.

'Anybody over twenty-five,' Ringo said. 'That's when the rot sets in.'

'The only rot I see around here is you,' Don Camillo shouted, 'and the human garbage you have with you, good-for-nothings wasting your lives shouting nonsense and listening to silly songs. You avoid every human responsibility and live scrounging off people or robbing your rotten parents of their small change.'

Ringo took a step towards Don Camillo. 'Look, I don't have any respect for your cassock or for your old age. The only reason I won't beat you up is because I pity you.'

'An honourable sentiment which, I'm sorry to say, doesn't touch my rotten but hard heart,' Don Camillo answered, coming down the embankment at a dead run.

Ringo was a boxer, and knew judo and karate, but Don Camillo's first two swings caught him on the ears and made him forget everything, including his own name and address. Grabbing his hair with both hands, Don Camillo hoisted him over his right shoulder, and started to beat him up. Flora's voice stopped him. 'Uncle, don't! Let Venom scalp him!'

'Young people are entitled to some rights,' Don Camillo admitted, dropping the bundle of flesh and climbing back up the embankment.

'If you weren't such pitiful slobs,' Don Camillo thundered from the ridge, 'if you were raising a real protest against our putrid world, instead of playing at cowboys and Indians, you'd do something constructive, like helping out flood victims who've lost everything.'

'I hope the flood victims all drop dead!' Ringo shouted as he stood up.

'They *will* all drop dead if some real rebel doesn't help them,' Don Camillo answered.

It was the second day of a flood that had ruined a third of the province, and the flood refugees, clustering like chickens atop the roofs of the submerged houses, were waiting and hoping that someone would remember them and come to their aid.

'That's real rebellion and protest!' Don Camillo went on. 'Protest against the politicians who are trying to solve the problem with speeches, protest against television broadcasts who are making a fine TV spectacular out of the whole thing to entertain all the bourgeois tubs wallowing in their armchairs and their selfishness. To jump in and help those miserable souls just to thumb your noses at the politicians and petty bureaucrats: that would be the protest of real men!'

'And what do you suggest we do, for instance?' Ringo retorted. 'Swim over to the flood areas, seeing as the roads are flooded or washed away?'

'Not all of them,' Don Camillo answered. 'If the Mayor was on the ball, he'd collect warm clothes, blankets, food, and so on, load them on to a couple of barges, and send them over there where the river and sea have inundated the towns and fields.'

'Well, the Mayor is on the ball!' Peppone shouted.

'Yes, Comrade,' Don Camillo agreed, 'but to move an

inch, you need permission from the Kremlin or from Mao.'

'That's not it at all,' Peppone answered. 'The trouble is, you can't get anybody to part with anything any more. They've seen where their stuff winds up too often.'

'Not at all, Mayor,' Don Camillo insisted. 'If we swear we'll distribute the goods personally, they'll give.'

'What do you mean, "we"?'

'You and I. Anybody who won't trust a priest, will trust a comrade, and vice versa.'

Peppone turned to the longhairs. 'The chickens among you can hop on your tricycles and scamper home to listen to your protest songs on the record player. The rest can come with me.'

'Count me in,' Flora piped up. 'Me and Venom's gang.' She gave them a hard eye.

'I don't give a hoot about the flood, but since it involves faking somebody out, count me in too!'

'We're in,' the Scorpions said in chorus. 'It'll be a laugh to watch these Methuselahs mess up their own Florence Nightingale organization!'

The truce was signed, and when heads were counted, twenty longhairs from each gang were serviceable. What with broken heads, arms and legs, ten Scorpions and ten country toughs had to be sent to the hospital, though.

Peppone got out his lorry and, with Don Camillo at his side, he made the rounds of the entire community. The byword was 'No money, just clothes, blankets and food', which made sense, because a peasant would rather part with a sack of flour than a single lira. And everybody gave, because they all remembered vividly the flood that had struck their own town fifteen years before, and again two years before, and didn't forget that in spite of all the politicians' promises, they had had to get back on their feet by themselves. While the collection moved ahead, Bigio, Brusco and Smilzo, aided by the longhairs, mobilized the fleet.

They had two big motor barges, of the kind that is used to transport sand and gravel, as well as two barges which were pontooned together for use in ferrying lorries across the river, towed by a tugboat. They loaded the ferry with a lorry and a tractor with four-wheel drive to pull a harvest wagon. When the goods had been collected, they were carefully packed into waterproof plastic bags and loaded on to the four barges.

It was a monumental ordeal. Peppone commanded one of the barges, manned by Ringo's twenty Scorpions; the other barge, commanded by Don Camillo, was filled with the twenty country boys and Flora.

Don Chichi was keen to go on the expedition, but Don Camillo reminded him that somebody had to stay behind and take care of the parish. 'And besides,' he added wisely, 'there's already me on this jaunt, and it's never wise to overdo it with priests.'

The fleet set off shortly after midnight, in the rain. The crews were covered with bruises and dead tired, so, taking refuge under the waterproof shrouds, they were soon fast asleep. Don Camillo's barge was the flagship, followed by Peppone's and the pontoon ferry towed by the tugboat. A small, swift outboard equipped with a bank of powerful searchlights led the way.

At about ten in the morning, the rain stopped and the weather cleared up a little. Naturally Don Camillo took advantage of this: in any case, it was Sunday. He had arranged a pile of crates full of canned food, and on top of this, he spread out his portable altar and began to celebrate Mass.

On Peppone's barge, the entire crew was still under the shroud, fast asleep.

'A typical priest!' Peppone growled. 'Any occasion is good for the old Music Hall performance!'

Ringo started to snigger, but the motors on all the barges had been cut off, and in that desolate spot the priest's words swelled out over the endless waste of muddy water into the silence, and Ringo didn't feel like sniggering any more.

A longhair without a guitar is like a soldier going into battle without a rifle, so naturally the Scorpions had their guitars with them, and when it came time for the Elevation, they sang *Old Man River*. During Communion, they hummed a mournful rock tune.

'Dear Lord,' Don Camillo muttered, 'why don't you make them shut up? Why don't you stop them from desecrating this holy moment with those profane songs of theirs?'

'Don Camillo,' the distant voice of the Christ answered, 'each of them is singing the praises of the Lord as best he can.'

'That may be, sir, but listen to them now: they're whistling!'

'On certain occasions, praises to the Lord may also be whistled,' the Christ explained.

'Dear Lord, where will all this end? Who could have imagined a poor country priest celebrating a rock Mass?'

'I could have, Don Camillo,' the Christ answered.

When the Mass was ended, the rain began anew. The motors were started up and everybody took shelter under the shrouds.

They finally came to the flooded lands in the Delta, and at the first sight of the roofs of the submerged houses, their troubles began.

It was the moment of coordinating forces. The co-ordinators sent by the government arrived to coordinate the rescue operations and to decide who would do what. The supervisors arrived shortly thereafter, to coordinate the coordinators.

Meanwhile the people, herded together on the roof-tops, waited.

A launch packed with officials and guardsmen halted the barges. 'Who are you? What are you doing here? Whose group do you belong to? What are you carrying? Why are you bringing this stuff, nobody asked for it.'

'What's going to happen is that they'll give us a fine because we don't have bills of lading from the Bureau of Commerce!' Flora muttered angrily.

'Keep quiet,' Don Camillo answered. 'Don't you understand that government efficiency hates private efficiency?'

The longhairs were getting annoyed. Ringo suggested scuttling the government launch and throwing the officials and guardsmen into the water. It was a good idea, but there was no need to put it into effect. Taking their own time about it, the coordinators decided they had held up the rescue operation for a respectable interval and churned off, allowing the flotilla to move forward again.

The longhairs helped people down from the rooftops into the barges. They ferried the poor souls over to the high land, dried them off, gave them warm clothes and something to eat; then, using the lorry and tractor, they transported them to towns spared from the flood. Each person received a supply of food, a blanket and warm clothes.

The last operation of the day was the Red House Rescue. The cottage was flooded almost as far as the first floor ceiling, and a little old man and woman had found safety on the sun roof, with all their worldly goods. They didn't want to abandon their house and possessions. Pleading and reasoning with them was useless, so Peppone cut it short and gave an order to Ringo: 'Gather up those two old fools and their knick-knacks and pile them into the barge.'

The Scorpions loved violence and obeyed without argument, deaf to the protests of the two old people.

The barge had only moved a few yards away from the cottage when the pathetic structure gave out a groan and disappeared into the muddy water. 'See there!' the old man crowed bitterly. 'That should make you all happy!'

'You're the ones who should be happy!' Ringo shouted in anger. 'If we'd waited two minutes longer to save you, you'd both be drowned now!'

'Exactly,' the old lady wailed. 'Then it would all be over. Now we're forced to go on living without a house or a garden or a chicken coop.'

'The government will help you,' Ringo said.

'The government,' the old man growled. 'The government will lock us up in an old people's home, me in one wing, her in another. We'll be apart for the rest of our lives, while we might have been able to die together, there in our own house!'

'What garbage!' Ringo sneered. 'Dying alone or in a crowd is dying all the same.'

'Young man,' the old man said, 'you have your whole life before you, we have ours behind us. At a certain point – and you'll see this – the problem is not how to live well, but how to die well.'

The two barges were alongside each other and Don Camillo spoke loud and clear: 'My dear man, I understand you but those young people can't possibly. They couldn't care less how old people die. All they want is for us to die off as soon as possible.'

'Then why didn't they leave us where we were?' the old lady wailed.

'Well if you're so anxious to die, nobody's stopping you from jumping overboard!'

'Only He who gave us life can take it away,' the old woman answered.

'Maybe you don't know that, young man, but the Father does,' the old man added.

'Fire up the engines!' Don Camillo called out. 'Mission accomplished, let's go home!'

'Aren't we going to get rid of them?' Peppone asked under his breath.

'We're responsible for their sad plight. I'll take them to that old manor house I bought; it's pretty run down, but some of the rooms are habitable. And besides, there's good land around it; we can clean it up for them and they can plant a garden and put in a chicken coop.'

The old woman's eyes lit up. 'A chicken coop!' she

exclaimed. But suddenly she was sad again. 'My poor chickens, all drowned . . .'

'Spanish galleon off the port bow!' Flora shouted.

A fair-sized block of filthy debris was floating along giving off vapours in the muddy water. Atop the heap, twenty or so chickens were mournfully pecking at the dung. 'Bengal tigers coming aboard!' Flora called out.

They pulled the dungheap alongside with grappling hooks and the chickens were loaded on board.

'Now you've even got your chickens,' Ringo roared. 'What more can you ask?'

'For the help of the Good Lord,' the old woman said, spreading out her arms.

'You'll have to try the shop next door,' the youth snarled. 'We don't cut any ice with Jesus Christ.'

The motors roared loudly and Don Camillo couldn't hear him. The Christ did, but He let it go. Deep down inside, he had been a longhair too, and He'd made a lot of people angry enough at His protest to crucify him.

And this is another of the stories the great river will tell to anybody who comes to listen to fables from the river's edge or the boat deck.

Two robbers turn into three

THESE were prosperous times. Impossible to discover why, but it was a brilliant feat: people worked less and less while they earned more and more. With prosperity came a wave of innovations: cabarets, discothèques, strip joints, whiskey-a-gogos, dirty films, rock music, soul music, even rock and soul Masses.

Women didn't breast-feed their babies any more but fed them preparations out of tins. There were frozen foods, hamburgers and hot-dogs, cold cuts, French fried potatoes. Prosperity required that every family buy a house with areas set aside for every activity, a car which had to be kept up, a television set, an enormous quantity of electrical appliances; it required them to escape from their many-area-ed houses every week-end, to spend their summer holiday by the sea, in the mountains, on a cruise.

All lovely things, but they cost a lot of money. Therefore, anybody who worked for a living was forced to strike often for higher pay. Anybody who didn't have a job made do in various ways. For example, you could pull a nylon stocking over your face and hold up jewellery stores, banks, and post offices.

Just before Christmas, because prosperity required considerable extra expenses during that season, the robberies increased. Thus it was that late one afternoon, just as the postmaster in Don Camillo's town was about to close up shop, two thugs with black neckerchiefs covering their faces appeared before him.

The bigger of the two planted himself in front of the cashier's window, forcing the postmaster to pretend he was writing something, while the other thug emptied the safe in a few seconds. Then both thugs ran out, jumped on their motorcycles parked on the street beside the post office, and disappeared.

The poor postmaster was left speechless for a few minutes. Fortunately, however, he hadn't lost his sight or hearing, and was able to ascertain that the two thugs were two longhairs named Ringo and Lucky. In the excitement of the hold-up they had spoken to each other by name, Ringo being the one with the black mop, while Lucky's was carrot-red. Furthermore, he managed to read the licence plates on their motorcycles.

It didn't take a squad of Pinkerton detectives to figure out that 'Ringo' was the notorious chief of the Scorpion gang, or that 'Lucky' was his first lieutenant. And as if that weren't sufficient evidence, Ringo and Lucky had dropped out of sight.

The police knew all about the Scorpions and they decided that the fact that Ringo's girlfriend lived in the town was of some interest. So they were off in a flash to pick up Flora. The girl, smelling smoke, had run to hide under Don Camillo's wing, and it was there that the police found her.

'You're Ringo's girlfriend,' the police chief asserted. 'Let's go down to the station, dear.'

'In the first place,' Flora said calmly, 'I am a tax-paying, voting adult and you will not use that tone in speaking to me again. In the second place, I haven't had anything to do with Ringo or his gang for some time now. I sell electrical appliances under licence from the Chamber of Commerce and can account for every move I make. And lastly, I don't understand why you're looking for those two boys. The Scorpions have never stolen from anybody.'

The police chief knew all about it and wasn't impressed. 'Well it's odd then,' he answered sarcastically, 'that the two thieves called each other Ringo and Lucky, had black and red hair like Ringo and Lucky, and rode Ringo's and Lucky's motorcycles.'

'Well it's even odder that they didn't leave autographed pictures behind at the post office, and odder still that, having gone to all that trouble to make sure you knew who they were, they haven't given themselves up,' Flora retorted.

'All right,' the chief roared, 'where are Ringo and Lucky then? Why have they disappeared?'

'Ask the police, who know everything. I'm just a poor girl who sells electrical appliances,' Flora said.

'That's enough!' the chief said nastily. 'You come along with us: we'll continue this conversation down at my place of business.'

Don Camillo stepped in. 'Captain, I'm the girl's uncle,' he said. 'If you want to beat her up, you're perfectly welcome to do it here.'

'Father!' the chief protested. 'We don't beat anybody up and we certainly don't intend to treat your niece in such a brutal fashion!'

'Too bad,' Don Camillo sighed, genuinely disappointed. 'A chance like this won't come again in my lifetime.'

They took Flora away at nine in the morning, aı. l a taxi brought her back at nine that night.

'How did it go?' Don Camillo inquired.

'Well, holy reverend Uncle,' Flora answered, 'I'll admit to you that once they really did scare me.'

'What's that? But you didn't have anything to do with it, did you?'

'That's precisely why. How can an innocent person defend himself? The truth's always too boring to convince anybody. If you don't tell a pack of lies, it's a sure thing you won't be able to get out of it.'

'And so you told a pack of lies?' Don Camillo shouted.

'Of course: how else was I to prove I was telling the truth?'

'You idiot! You'll see, they'll be after you.'

'I should hope so,' Flora answered. 'I sold them a fridge, two washing machines, a dishwasher, and a floor polisher. But I'm still worried about Ringo and Lucky, poor kids.'

'You have the cheek to feel sorry for those two long-haired thieves?'

Flora shook her head. 'Holy reverend Uncle, you missed your calling. You should have been a policeman. You're just the right size. And apart from everything else, a bad priest is worse than a bad policeman.'

Things began to happen around two in the morning. Somebody tapped on Don Camillo's bedroom window with a pole; Don Camillo, seeing who it was, took down his shotgun and went to open the door.

Dragging two beat-up bicycles, Ringo and Lucky came into the rectory. They were much the worse for wear, odoriferous and quite black-and-blue. Don Camillo didn't let go of the shotgun and demanded inhospitably, 'Why did you come here?'

'*Pulsate et aperietur vobis*,' Ringo said with a tired smile. 'We're cold, hungry, and bone-tired. It's been four days and nights that we've had to lie low and live off the land like dogs.'

'Like wolves, not dogs!' Don Camillo snapped. 'Anyhow, my only duty is to call up the police.'

'All right,' Ringo said bitterly. 'We haven't even got the strength to climb back on our bikes. At least give us something to eat.'

'You'll get something down at the gaol,' Don Camillo said, moving towards the telephone.

'Don't waste your time, holy reverend Uncle,' said a voice from behind him. 'I've cut the wires.'

Flora, all decked out for the occasion, came into the

159

room and planted herself between Don Camillo's shotgun and the two longhairs.

'I'll give them something to eat,' she said. 'My pickup's right inside the woodshed. Get it out, you two. And then wait inside it.'

'Flora,' Don Camillo croaked, 'remove yourself from the middle of this. Don't get mixed up with those two thugs.'

'I'm no fat old priest dying of sleep and fear,' the girl answered. 'Before I condemn people, I want to hear what they have to say.'

'Forget it, Flora,' Ringo said. 'He's right, you shouldn't get mixed up in this. Just give us a piece of bread and something to put over our shoulders, and we'll hit the road.'

The two longhairs were truly pathetic-looking, and Don Camillo felt like an idiot with his shotgun. To make matters sillier, the perfidious Flora had sneaked up and clasped her hand over the muzzle of the shotgun. Don Camillo pulled the gun away from her and propped it up in a corner.

'Light the fire and make them something to eat,' he said. 'Not even I can condemn a person without listening to them first. But I can't imagine what these two criminals will have to say.'

'Well for one thing, we didn't have anything to do with that robbery,' Ringo said as a log began to burn in the huge fireplace. 'Some son of a gun framed us. They swiped our motorcycles and made the whole thing look as if we'd done it.'

'Just what I told the police,' Flora said, bringing in bread, salami, and wine.

'Nonsense!' Don Camillo declared. 'If so, you would have reported the theft to the police and you wouldn't be in trouble now.'

The warmth and wine had restored the two longhairs' strength. Ringo sneered. 'Are you kidding? The head of the Scorpions and his second-in-command let their cycles disappear right out from under their noses, then they go whimper about it to the police – like two middle-class mamma's boys! Please! We have some self-respect. Apart from the fact that we haven't got much faith in your rotten system of justice. The only justice we believe in is what we make for ourselves. This is between the Scorpions and whoever those two crooks were.'

'Three,' Flora amended. 'It's obvious: two of them pulled off the hold-up and met a third who was waiting for them in a car. They ditched the bikes and drove off calm as could be in the car. Only a stupid policeman or a priest wouldn't be able to see how simple the thing is.'

Don Camillo had a great deal of respect for the forces of law and order, but it annoyed him to be compared to a stupid policeman. He studied the two longhairs in confusion. He had seen them risk their skins to save flood victims. With those long, dishevelled mops, unsightly beards, and filthy, torn clothes they looked like two brigands. But ordinarily, he thought, brigands don't look at all like brigands.

'And who's to assure me that's the way it happened?' Don Camillo growled.

'We are,' the two answered.

'That's not good enough,' Don Camillo said. 'I need some guarantee that you're not telling me a pack of lies just to show you don't fear God.'

'That's not true,' Ringo protested. 'God has His problems, and we have ours; peaceful coexistence.'

'If you don't mind, I'd like to have just one thing straight,' Don Camillo exclaimed in exasperation. 'Do you or don't you believe in God?'

Ringo laughed. 'If we denied the existence of God, we'd deny our own existence and that of the entire universe. We're rebels, but we're protesting and rebelling against men, not God.'

Don Camillo was a typical product of the operatic nation and never missed a chance for a good theatrical scene. 'Follow me!' he thundered, moving off.

The church, illuminated only by a few votive candles, was full of deep, chilly mystery. He stopped in front of the ancient high altar.

'Make the sign of the cross!' he ordered the two boys. They obeyed.

'Do you swear to Christ on the cross that you are completely innocent of that robbery?'

'We swear it,' the two said without wavering.

They all trailed back to the rectory fireplace. 'Wasn't their word of honour good enough for you?' Flora stormed. 'Do you believe a person couldn't perjure himself in front of an old stick of wood?'

'Of course that's possible,' Don Camillo admitted gloomily. 'But anybody who tried it would be starting something with God. It's one thing to fool a poor country priest, and it's quite another to try to fool God.'

'We're not trying to fool anybody,' Ringo said. 'Well, what do we do now?'

'For the time being, you stay here. And not in those foul clothes. I'll buy you some decent clothes and cut your hair.'

'Forget the business about cutting our hair,' Ringo snapped.

'But don't you realize that if anybody sees you with those mops, the game's up immediately, and we're all in trouble?'

'We understand, all right,' Ringo answered. 'Thanks for the hospitality. Rather than cut our hair, we'll turn ourselves in!'

Don Camillo came up with a compromise: he would lock them in the room at the top of the bell tower.

'What about Don Chichi?' Flora asked, worried. 'That one sticks his nose in everywhere, and he'll find them there.'

'He won't find them because I'm going to tell him about them first,' Don Camillo reassured her.

'Will he rat on us?' Ringo asked nervously.

'No,' Don Camillo said. 'All I have to do is make him

believe you're the two real crooks and you did it to spite society. He'll defend you to the death. The important thing is not to let him suspect you're innocent.'

'Don't you worry about it, reverend Uncle,' Flora said laughing. 'I'll explain everything to Don Chichi. I know all the ins and outs with these progressive priests. And I'll think the rest of it through too. When the postmaster gave the alarm, the cops set up road blocks all around the area but didn't spot any motorcycles. That means the two bikes should be somewhere near town. What we have to do is find them.'

Flora mobilized Venom's gang and gave them clear orders: 'Get going and find two bikes. If you find them, don't touch them, just stand guard and send somebody for me.'

The great river had exhausted its fit of bad temper: it had come as far as the top of the embankment and dikes, licked them, and then retreated. A little path led down from the embankment ridge to a level place near the water's edge, and there two motorcycles blossomed from the mud. Flora notified the police, who went to collect them. They were the two motorcycles used in the hold-up, and inside the saddlebags were two wigs, one black and one red, two pistols, and two black neckerchiefs.

Don Camillo brought the news to the bell tower.

Ringo laughed. 'Reverend, if we'd let you chop off our hair, what a mess we'd be in now if they found us!'

The next day, a stolen car was found on the outskirts of town, and inside it were the documents that the thieves had taken from the post office safe in their rush to filch the money. During the get-away, the car had to be re-fuelled and the garage man at Castelletto remembered the occupants of the car very well. They were three well-known professional crooks from the city. They were hunted down and made to confess. The story appeared in minute detail on the front page of the newspapers.

'Now then,' Don Camillo said to the two longhairs, who by then had been allowed to come downstairs, 'you can go over to the police station and clear things up with them in peace and quiet.'

Ringo shook his head. 'Let the cops clear up their own filthy messes. We have an account to settle with the crooks who pulled that dirty trick on us. We know who they are now, but they don't know Ringo and Lucky. They'll find out soon enough.'

'What are you going to do, break into gaol and beat them up?' Don Camillo asked.

'It's only a matter of a few months' patience,' Ringo said. 'When the next amnesty comes round, we'll be waiting to do them up good and proper when they come out.'

But there was Don Chichi, who stepped in righteously.

'Boys, you must not do this! Remember that those three unfortunates are victims of social injustice and their act was a justifiable demonstration of rebellion against the selfishness of the rich!'

'What's this, the Eleventh Commandment?' Ringo sneered. 'In any case, don't you worry. We'll use a nice gentle stick to break their bones with.'

'It's a kind thought,' Don Camillo admitted. 'It would be an even sweeter thought if, before you left, you'd step into the church to give thanks to God for helping you out.'

'That's not necessary,' Ringo answered. 'We'll take care of that when we get back to the base. There's a God in the city too, you know.'

That was a comforting bit of news and it cheered Don Camillo up considerably.

Epilogue

PEPPONE was so infuriated that at a poke of the finger he would have given off sparks. Up until a certain time, Peppone and his high command had ruled the town uncontested because the Communists and Socialists combined amounted to double plus one the number of Social-Democrats and clergy. Then the comrades of the La Rocca faction set up their autonomous Maoist cell headed by the young fanatic Doctor Bognoni, who as a town councillor disagreed with Peppone's group right down the line.

After the flood, the Socialists regrouped into a party which also included the clergy, leaving Peppone and his comrades isolated, with a block of votes exactly equal to that of the Socialist-clergy unit. That left Bognoni's wife, the pharmacist, as the arbiter of the situation, since her single vote could sway the balance of power one way or the other.

And since the sins of children are always visited on their fathers, the young Mrs Bognoni, who had once been mortified when Venom forced her to drink half a bottle of cod-liver oil, now got a great deal of pleasure from standing in the way of any project Peppone suggested.

Peppone put up a good fight for a while, then decided to let Socialists, clergy and pharmacists pave the road to hell for themselves. The world doesn't come to an end if a mayor resigns; but Peppone was a special kind of mayor.

He had taken the tiller of the rocky township during the stormy post-war period, and while flying the red flag, had managed to keep the little boat on a straight course. For that reason, when election time came round, even those who saw Communism as the path to perdition voted unhesitatingly for Peppone.

When people heard via the grapevine that Peppone wanted to resign, they began to worry. Two industrialists from the outside had decided to build a plywood mill and a plastics factory; they had already begun to excavate foundations for the buildings on the property allotted to them by the community, but they stopped construction and went home. The owner of an agricultural equipment business immediately began to move his establishment to a less explosive community.

So Don Camillo buttonholed Peppone and tried to persuade him to change his mind. 'Comrade, it wasn't the Party who gave you your job, it was the majority of the voters.'

'The majority may propose, but the Party disposes,' Peppone replied. 'I can't put myself at the mercy of a silly young woman.'

Peppone, when he'd made up his mind, went ahead like a tank, and any fool knows how hard it is to argue with a tank.

Don Camillo visited the pharmacy to try and persuade the Red Guard pharmacist to end her revolution and come back into the fold. The lady Maoist's lip curled. 'The mere fact that a priest was sent here to talk to me proves that Peppone has betrayed the Leninist ideal and the working class. Why don't you hire him as sexton?'

When they dabble in politics, women are even harder to reason with than tanks, and Don Camillo didn't waste his time arguing with her. He went straight to Belicchi, a Socialist who up until very recently had been an ally of Peppone's. Belicchi heard Don Camillo out, then replied with thinly disguised disgust: 'It's absolutely shameful, a priest trying to help out the Communists.'

'I'm trying to help us have a good town administration,' Don Camillo answered.

'The hell with the town administration,' Belicchi declared. 'The only thing that matters is the Party.'

'Too bad the sewage system doesn't know anything about politics. Otherwise the sewage would be able to make its way out of town without complicated piping. What about the two factories? And the farm equipment manufacturer? That's work for two thousand labourers right there.'

Belicchi just laughed. 'Better to have two thousand unemployed workers than pander to three filthy industrialists. When we come to power, we'll set everything right with industrial planning.'

Socialists are very hard-headed, so Don Camillo crossed his arms and said, 'Can I ask just one question?'

'Certainly.'

'What would you say if one of these nights somebody stepped out of the shadows and belted you over the head?'

Belicchi burst out laughing. 'Father, Peppone doesn't scare anybody any more. The Communists have all gone bourgeois.'

'But I haven't,' Don Camillo pointed out.

'You'd beat me up on Peppone's account?'

'No, on my own account, Comrade Belicchi. Once upon a time when I was a leftist priest like Don Chichi, you were running around in a black shirt and one night you stepped out of the shadows and belted me over the head. I can always get even with you. And all by myself, without three thugs to back me up like you had.'

Belicchi waved him off impatiently. 'Father, don't be childish. That was centuries ago. Who remembers it?'

'I do,' Don Camillo answered. 'While the ambusher may have a short memory, it doesn't necessarily follow that his victim is as forgetful.'

'But I was just a boy and I redeemed myself fighting in the Resistance!'

'I'll bear that in mind. I won't beat up an ex-partisan but rather an ex-Fascist.'

Don Camillo had picked Belicchi up by his lapels, and the man went white. 'You can't do this to me! Everybody knows now that I was a double agent!'

'My head doesn't know it,' Don Camillo explained as he began to bounce Belicchi off the wall.

'All right, all right, what do you want me to do?' the poor man stammered.

'Leave the Socialists and go back with the Communists,' Don Camillo proposed.

'Is it really you asking me such a thing? You, a priest?'

'As far as I'm concerned, all you Marxists are all going to hell anyway,' Don Camillo answered. 'It makes no difference to me whether you fry in a pan or boil in a kettle.'

Don Camillo had some very persuasive arguments and Belicchi decided to leave the frying pan and move into the kettle. This gave Peppone a clear majority and the pharmacist's vote against him was reduced to a pitiful bow in Mao's direction.

Naturally, Don Camillo had worked as secretly as possible and, taking advantage of a reunion to protest against the war in Vietnam, Peppone showed his gratitude to Don Camillo by delivering a round denunciation of priestly machinations to undermine the democratic system of town elections. It was a fierce, articulate attack that left Don Camillo with his mouth wide open.

He and Flora listened to the broadcast of the speech together, and afterward he exclaimed: 'I can't understand how that devil came to put a speech like that together!'

'He only read it. He gave me a few general ideas and I wrote it for him,' Flora explained, with that diabolical smile of hers.

'So! And where did you manage to dig up all those quotes from Saint Paul, Saint Augustine, Saint Thomas, the *Rerum Novarum*, and Pope John?'

'Well, Don Chichi has to serve some useful purpose', Flora said.

'You wretch,' Don Camillo shouted, 'are you turning against me again?'

'Not at all, holy reverend Uncle, I'm just giving a hand to the future grandfather of my children.'

Don Camillo eyed the girl pityingly. 'And you really think that boy is stupid enough to marry you?'

'What's he got to do with it? *I'm* marrying *him*!'

'Tell me this: does he know you've decided to marry him?'

'Of course. I wrote him about it and he answered that he'd be delighted.'

'Lies! I won't admit there's a man in the world *that* dimwitted. Not unless you read me his answer.'

'Technically impossible,' Flora explained calmly. 'The post was on strike and so as not to lose time, I took the letter to him personally and he answered verbally.'

Don Camillo jumped. 'You'd even do that! And your mother says it's all right?'

'My mother?' The girl tittered. 'You mean that boring woman who does nothing but gossip all day long or remind me of all the things I shouldn't be doing?'

'Don't be a comic! Does your mother know or doesn't she that you're going to get married?'

'I suppose eventually she'll find out about it too, there are so many chatterboxes in this world.'

Don Camillo was seized with the urge to pick Flora up and bounce *her* off the wall. 'So it's come to this!' he shouted. 'Now girls get married without even letting their mothers know!'

'I suppose she let *me* know when she was getting married.' The shameless girl giggled and then added, 'Mind you, Uncle, I'm getting married in a miniskirt, like it or not!'

'Like it or not, you'll come into my church decently dressed and with your face washed!' Don Camillo retorted.

'Imagine me turning up dressed like some Daughter of Mary in front of the boys.'

'Don't worry about the boys. There aren't going to be any of those loudmouthed longhairs around. Even if people are trying to turn marriage into some kind of side-show, it's still a serious business.'

Flora lost her temper. 'I mean to get married dressed exactly as I see fit, and I mean to invite my own guests. Either that, or I get married in the town hall!'

'Child,' Don Camillo said, waving a foot at her, 'you see I wear a size twelve shoe. Well, if you're not out of here in five seconds, you'll feel it!'

The girl scooted out like a rabbit.

That seemed to be the end of the discussion, but a week later the subject of Flora's wedding came up again, and it was Don Chichi who raised it.

'Father, your niece is an impulsive girl but she has common sense at least. She's thought it over: she'd like a wedding blessed by God, but naturally she wants it to have the stamp of her own unique personality too.'

'What does *that* mean?'

'She's a skydiver, he's a Paratrooper. They'll say their vows just after they jump. There's already been a wedding like it, so you don't have to worry about setting a precedent. I think it's a fine idea! Think of it, that solemn promise made far above the uglinesses of earthly life, way up there in the free sky. Closer to God.'

'I see,' Don Camillo growled. 'I suppose the priest marries them from down below, watching through binoculars?'

'Not at all, the priest jumps with them! Tomorrow I'm starting a course in skydiving.'

'I see,' Don Camillo growled louder, 'Flora's managed to con you.'

'I *want* to do it,' Don Chichi exclaimed. 'Think of it. A group of friends from the groom's squadron will partici-pate in the rite and jump along with them. I can see those great white flowers blossoming against the bright blue sky now! Yes, even progress has its poetry. I'll set up my field altar in the landing area and celebrate Mass there in a skydiving suit! Believe me, Father: in this manner too the Church will go on updating and renewing itself and adapting to progress!'

Don Camillo nodded solemnly. 'It will be an epoch-making Mass.'

Don Camillo didn't see Flora for a month. 'You see, Uncle,' she said cheerfully, 'we'll be able to eat our cake and have it too. We'll have a proper Catholic wedding, without being trite about it. Don Chichi is a treasure: he's already made his first jump. He's coming along just fine and I'm sure he'll be ready for the big day. That's the way priests should be today – modern and dynamic. To make the ceremony more impressive, we'll jump from seventy-five hundred feet. We'll dive for six thousand feet holding hands and we'll have plenty of time to say "I do". At fifteen hundred feet, Don Chichi opens his chute and pulls away. At twelve hundred feet, Venom opens up, and at nine hundred, I do.'

'It would be much more impressive if *you* didn't open your chute at all,' Don Camillo growled. 'That moron who's marrying you, does he agree to all this?'

'Of course.'

'You're having the witnesses jump too?'

'Naturally! Venom's quite prepared because his witnesses are his lieutenant and another man from the troop. My witnesses are going to be Lucky, the Scorpions' second-in-command, and Speedy, Venom's second-in-command, and they're taking skydiving lessons now.'

Venom finished his stint in the army and as soon as he arrived home he went over to the rectory with Flora. He was clearly embarrassed.

'Father,' he stammered, 'your niece and I would like to get married.'

'I know,' Don Camillo replied. 'I'm sorry I won't be able to perform the ceremony myself. The fact is, at my age I don't feel like taking a dive from seventy-five hundred feet.'

Venom shot a questioning look at Flora and then said, 'What's this business about diving from seventy-five hundred feet?'

'We'll discuss it later,' Flora said swiftly. 'Anyhow, Father, can you perform the stunt pretty soon, or do we have to go through a *Promessi Sposi* type engagement?'

'If the Department of Health doesn't put you away in a bin before the time, the two of you could make the greatest mistake of your lives in eight days.'

Venom was back three days later. 'Can you marry us here, in your church, Saturday morning?' he asked.

'Certainly,' Don Camillo answered. 'Are the bride's witnesses still going to be Lucky and Speedy?'

'For the moment, yes,' Venom said gloomily. 'But there are still five days left.'

Venom was nervous as a cat and his right cheek was scarred with a deep scratch, so Don Camillo didn't ask any more questions.

That Saturday morning, when Don Camillo entered the church through the sacristy, he found the church packed with people. His heart almost failed when he spotted Flora marching forward to the altar on the arm of her father's brother. Not only that, but, praise be to God, she wasn't wearing a miniskirt but a long white dress that seemed to trail off to infinity. To compensate, Venom's left cheek was scarred with an even deeper scratch.

But Don Camillo completely lost his breath when Flora's witnesses marched up. Dressed in impeccable morning suits and their hair neatly trimmed, Lucky and Speedy were quite a pair.

'Our wedding present to Flora,' Lucky whispered, pointing to his head.

Don Camillo felt a shiver go up his spine when he thought what that gift must have cost the two young men.

But the most frightening moment for Don Camillo came when it was time for her to say 'I do'. 'Dear Lord, please keep one hand on the girl's brow. If I know her, just to spite me she'll say "I don't".'

'Don't give it a thought,' the distant voice of the Christ answered.

And sure enough, Flora said 'I do' loud and clear.

At that precise instant Don Chichi, profoundly embittered but always a die-hard, jumped from seventy-five hundred feet. It was a perfect jump but at a low altitude a nasty little breeze whipped up and wrapped the parachute around the top of a tall poplar, and his lines got so tangled that the fire brigade had to use an extension ladder to pick Don Chichi out of the tree.

But he was left hanging for quite a while, and his only consolation was to see Flora's and Venom's car speed by on the road below and turn off towards the highway, followed by eighty assorted longhairs on motorcycles.

All of which goes to prove that even if a priest is perched on a poplar, all psalms end in glory.

Penguinews *and* Penguins in Print

Every month we issue an illustrated magazine, *Penguinews*. It's a lively guide to all the latest Penguins, Pelicans and Puffins, and always contains an article on a major Penguin author, plus other features of contemporary interest.

Penguinews is supplemented by *Penguins in Print*, a complete list of all the available Penguin titles – there are now over four thousand!

The cost is no more than the postage; so why not write for a free copy of this month's *Penguinews*? And if you'd like both publications sent for a year, just send us a cheque or a postal order for 30p (if you live in the United Kingdom) or 60p (if you live elsewhere), and we'll put you on our mailing list.

Dept EP, Penguin Books Ltd,
Harmondsworth, Middlesex

Note: *Penguinews* and *Penguins in Print* are not available in the U.S.A. or Canada.

Also by Giovanni Guareschi

The Little World of Don Camillo

This classic of humour was Guareschi's first report
from the Little World down in the Valley of the Po,
where the Good Lord strives to keep the peace
between Don Camillo, the honest village priest, and
Peppone, the Communist mayor, his venomous
opponent.

The House that Nino Built

CHAOTIC like the time they replanned the new
house and ended up with a 15-inch door on each
side of the flue . . . UPROARIOUS like the time the
front gate became an assault course . . . BARMY like
the time the Red Duchess (rising seven) went on
strike up the apple tree . . . EVEN SENTIMENTAL
like the time Margherita went in search of her lost
youth – and Nino was the soul of tact . . .

If you've got a family, it'll delight you. If you
haven't, it'll make you want to start one.

Not for sale in the U.S.A. or Canada